My Summer With The King

By: Melissa Goodman

# INTRODUCTION

Most epic novels have a great opening line like Moby Dick's "Call me Ishmael." I've never read the book but that one line almost convinces me to give it a go. Another favorite of mine is Gone With the Wind's "Scarlett O'Hara was not beautiful, but men seldom seemed to realize it when caught by her charms as the Tarleton twins were." I first read Margaret Mitchell's Pulitzer Prize winning book in 1953. That was the summer I turned 12. I remember that year clearly for that was when my life changed forever. Now that I've given you that little chunk to nibble on, I think it's time for my book to begin.

My name is May Richards. Growing up I despised the name. I thought it stupid to be named after a calendar month. A month I was not even born in mind you. My birthday is in July. I suffered much taunting from mean boys who asked where my sisters April and June were. But Momma Rose named me May and I never bothered to complain to her about it.

You see, complaining to Momma Rose failed to do any good. She believed in doing what needed to be done and with as little fuss as possible. Life was not good to her because of mistakes, missed chances, and lost opportunities. She could work, cuss, and drink any man under the table. Though she made many, many, many mistakes, she owned up to them and pushed on to the next. The biggest one being, according to her, was my daddy.

Momma Rose met Daddy during World War II. Being located close to Fort Knox, Louisville became filled with soldiers on leave. A fresh face eighteen year old, Momma Rose had gotten a job as a fountain manager at Tayler's Drug Store to support herself. Daddy was one of the thousand lonely soldiers who sat down at the counter. Momma claimed it was love at first sight for Daddy. It didn't surprise me. Momma Rose was unique-looking, if not traditionally beautiful with her long black hair and porcelain skin. But if you ask me, Daddy probably fell in love with Momma Rose's smile. When she smiled it lit up her entire face.

Daddy came back on each of his next two leaves and spent hours, not to mention his soldier's earnings, charming Momma Rose and coaxing her to go out with him. Her better sense tried to tell her no, but the handsome soldier boy with the sweet heart won in the end. They went to the picture show that night and walked the streets until dawn. Daddy regaling Momma with stories of camp and his family back in Ohio. Momma Rose enjoyed the attention, and by the time Daddy received his order to report to the Pacific they had married and I was on the way.

I don't remember much about my daddy. Most of my memories are, in all actuality, Momma Rose's. One of the good things I do recall is that Daddy would lift me as high as his two arms would stretch and would then crush me to his chest in a bear hug. If I live to be a hundred I would never forget the feeling of security and love there.

Momma Rose always claimed that she found me under a rock. I believed her until my sister Daisy was born when I was five. She was the prettiest baby I had ever seen and was a real live baby doll for me. Momma Rose said I fussed over her just like a mother hen. I don't remember it but I guess I felt I had to. After Daisy was born Momma and Daddy fought more. Then one morning I woke up and the fighting was done. Daddy was gone.

# CHAPTER TWO

In 1953, Momma Rose moved us into the house on Haywood Ave. There was nothing special about moving. We moved so much that six-year-old Daisy and I were professionals at it. My cousin Thelma liked to tease that we moved when the rent came due. At times that wasn't far from the truth.

I liked the house on Haywood. It resembled nothing of the one and two bedroom apartments that we were use to. The house was simple in design. It looked like every other house on the block with its fresh white paint and shotgun design. Nothing fancy but to people like us it might as well have been a mansion.

I never asked Momma Rose how she could afford the rent. Thelma told me that the rent was twenty five bucks a month which was steep for anyone not named Rockafeller in 1953. Momma Rose made it work though. Or rather she worked her fingers to the bone. She kept her job as the fountain manager and picked up a side job cleaning office buildings to make ends meet.

That did not leave her a lot for Daisy and me. We rarely saw Momma Rose during the week and were left mostly in the care of Thelma. Which is to say I took care of Daisy and Thelma did as she pleased. At sixteen, Thelma was cooler than Momma Rose. She never treated me like a kid.

A woman ahead of the 1960s sexual revolution, or just fast, as Momma Rose said, had no problem with straight talk. She was the one who told me where babies came from when I was ten. She gave me tips on how to handle boys who were fresh (at ten I had no idea what that meant) and all the social etiquette of parking. Next to Daisy, who at six was not as grown up as me, Thelma was my best friend. Despite her claims of popularity I think I was her best friend as well.

But more on Thelma later. We moved into the house on Haywood on a sunny afternoon in late May. After much debate, Momma Rose couldn't drive a stick, she somehow convinced my uncle Sonny to lend her his truck. Before he changed his mind she opened the passenger side door and told me to get in.

"It's not fair," I said, crossing my arms in front of me. "I want to sit by the window."

"You're the oldest, May. I expect better of you. Now go," Momma Rose said, pushing me toward the truck.

I stomped my feet but got in the truck anyway. Momma lifted a beaming Daisy in the seat beside me and shut the door.

"Ha, ha," Daisy said, sticking her tongue out at me.

"Momma," I exclaimed as she got in the truck and stared at the steering wheel.

"Not now, May. Can't you see I'm busy?"

I slumped down in the seat in a huff. It wasn't fair. I was the oldest. I deserved that window seat. Not content to let Daisy win, I reached over and pinched her on the arm. Daisy howled like I had shot her.

"For Christ's sake," Momma Rose yelled, "can't the two of you get along for two minutes?"

"May pinched me," Daisy said.

"I did not," I proclaimed my innocence even though the damning evidence was turning into a purple bruise.

Thankfully Momma Rose didn't bother to look over. Instead she turned the key and revved the engine to life. She battled with the clutch and the truck lurched forward. As she gave it a little gas we did the dance of start and stop. As Momma Rose pulled out into traffic, my fight with Daisy slipped away. I was less worried about the window seat and more concerned with surviving the ride. As a quiet Daisy placed her hand in mine I knew she was worried about the same thing.

As we made our way to the new house, horns blew and sped around us. It didn't bother Momma Rose until one angry-looking man in a Buick pulled up beside us.

"Leave the driving to your old man, sweetheart," the red-faced man screamed laying on his horn.

Momma Rose, never taking her eyes from the road, held her hand out the window. While I couldn't see it, experienced told me she gave him the one finger salute. "Kiss my ass, asshole."

The man in the Buick sped off but that was just the beginning of her tirade. No one ever called Momma Rose shy and she was at her worst when upset. Daisy and I had the most colorful vocabulary of any grade schoolers we knew. We used them in context and if there had been a cuss word spelling bee, I certainly would have won.

It wasn't until we pulled in front of the new house that Momma began to wind down and we got to see our new home for the first time. I admit I was surprised. It looked like a neighborhood from a television show. There were kids playing catch. Across the street a group of men Momma's age were huddled around a broken down jalopy. A gray-haired looking grandma peeked out of the curtain from the house next to us. A nice, normal neighborhood.

Right then the front door opened and Thelma came bouncing down the steps. I often wondered how someone always in such a rush seemed so put together. She wore denim pedal pushers and a white cotton blouse. Her onyx hair pulled tightly into a ponytail and her cheeks stained with rouge. Momma Rose didn't look happy.

"Have you done one thing I asked you to do?"

"I got distracted," Thelma said, looking past them. She smiled and gave a flirtatious wave of her fingers. "Hey boys."

We all looked across the street. The men had stopped working on the car and stared back at Thelma. They all looked older. Like I said, most looked to be closer to Momma Rose's thirty. But from the looks of it, none of them seemed to mind the age difference. Two had even made their way to the end of the driveway. Only one blond-haired man seemed not to notice.

Momma Rose placed her hand on her hips and called out, "She's sixteen."

"Aunt Rose, why did you do that? You're embarrassing me."

"A babe in your belly and no wedding ring would embarrass you a sight more. And from the looks of them that's all you're going to get."

"Excuse me, Ma'am," the younger of the two men interjected. He looked nice enough with his jeans and white t-shirt. He had a pack of cigarettes rolled up in one sleeve and another dangled from his fingertips.

"Yes," Momma Rose said in her clearly put out voice. The tone that Daisy and I got whenever we tugged on her skirt at the market.

"My name's Paul but my friends call me Buddy. JR and I meant no disrespect. We were just being friendly."

"Well Thelma doesn't need any more friends," she said, stressing the last word. She gathered Daisy's hand and headed up the walk. "Come along girls. We have work to do."

I grabbed a crate out of the back of the truck when one of the other men spoke.

"What about you?"

Momma Rose stopped and did a slow turn. It was the blond-haired man. He stood leaning against the car wiping oil from his hands. He was clearly the oldest of the men. Maybe a few years older than Momma Rose even. His hair was buzzed short. With the hair, stocky build, and cool demeanor I imagined he had to be in the military.

Momma Rose must have thought so too. "What about me, soldier?"

"Do you need any friends?" He put a similar emphasis on friends and caused his buddies to snicker.

Momma Rose looked at me and then down at Daisy. For the briefest of seconds I saw the loneliness there. Daisy was either too young or maybe she saw it as well because she beamed up her brightest smile at Momma. But Momma Rose didn't smile back. She steeled her back and looked at the man.

"Honey, I don't need anyone." *Especially from the likes of you*, hung in the air.

The man moved closer to stand with his buddies and smiled. With its perfectly aligned white teeth it was a nice smile. You know the type that you only saw in the movies. He leaned an elbow on JR's shoulder. "We've got us one of those independent women."

The other two men laughed.

Momma took the bait. She whipped around dragging Daisy with her. "Let me tell you something honey. You can call me anything you like. But its men like you who force me into it. A woman can't depend on a man these days. If she wants something she has to go out there and get it for herself."

"Cry me a river. You know you like being a ballbuster. You're probably raising these three to be just like you. Congratulations girls, you're going to be old and bitter."

That stopped Momma Rose in her tracks. Her face got red and I was convinced that the stranger was about to get a whaling of epic proportions. Imagine my disappointment when Momma Rose turned away and began pulling Daisy up the walk. I glanced at Thelma and she was just as disappointed as me. She shrugged and quickly followed after Momma.

That just left me standing there in the middle of the yard. The men laughed and joked about how the blond man had "got" Momma Rose. Eventually, JR and Buddy made their way back toward the car.

"What's your name girl?" the blond man asked.

I looked at him almost out of shock from being noticed. Before I opened my mouth our eyes met. I couldn't see it but instinctively knew there was a darkness to him. Something sinister, though I didn't know why I thought that. He didn't twirl a mustache (mainly I think because he did not have one) but I knew he was a villain.

"May, get your ass in here right now," Momma Rose called from inside the house.

I flew up the steps so fast I doubt my feet touched the ground. I caught the screen as it threatened to slam into the frame behind me. I chanced a look, and he was still there and still watching me. Then, with a nod of his head, he turned and strolled off.

I met three men that would forever change my life that summer. One that would change my way of thinking. One that would change my way of loving and this one…the one who destroyed my childhood.

# CHAPTER THREE

"May, can I ask you something?" Daisy asked the next morning as we sat rocking on the back porch swing. Momma Rose had already left for our old apartment to clean in hopes of getting the security deposit back. Thelma, who Momma left in charge, had been on the phone with her boyfriend Eddie ever since.

"I guess," I answered.

"Am I going to be old and bitter like that man said?"

"Of course you aren't. Well you will get old but not bitter."

"I don't want to get bitter."

"Do you even know what bitter means?"

"No," Daisy shook her head, "but it sure doesn't sound good."

I agreed. Daisy might have only been six but she was right on that one. The swing had come to a stop so I put my foot on the ground and sent it back into motion and set on trying to explain. "You know how Aunt Diane hates Momma Rose because great grandma liked momma better?"

"Yeah. Diane's mean."

"That's bitter," I waved my hands out like a magician for effect, "and you, dear sister, will never be like that. People love you."

My explanation seemed enough for Daisy. She was like that. Half the battle was making things logical for my sister. If you could give her a reason she'd accept it as the truth. For the most part, Daisy was a typical little sister. She cried and manipulated Momma Rose to get her way (read: my things). With her long dark hair and green eyes she was the prettier of us girls. Petite and skinny while I, at almost twelve, still had what people called "baby fat." On my best days I might be called cute, but Daisy was beautiful. People often stopped Momma Rose and asked if she entered Daisy in beauty pageants. Not once to my recollection had anyone said something like that about me.

Daisy was also smart. She loved to read. Momma Rose could not believe it when Daisy began reading at four. I was six when I started reading and in my opinion, a perfectly normal age. By now Daisy could read most adult books if she chose. In fact, at the end of the school year Mrs. Mumfort, Daisy's teacher, suggested that she skip the second grade all together. Momma Rose answered with an absolute no.

"My kids have enough strikes against them without adding freak to the list. Second grade is just dandy," Momma Rose replied when Mrs. Mumfort inquired why not.

Lost in our own thoughts both of us were silent for a minute. Daisy picked up her doll and begin picking at the hem of the doll's skirt. "I don't like that man."

She didn't have to tell me who. I knew exactly who she was talking about.

"Me neither."

"I think that Momma Rose likes him."

"Why do you say that?"

Daisy hugged her doll close to her chest. "I don't know. She didn't cuss at him."

She had me there. "But that doesn't mean she likes him."

"He also looks like Daddy."

I pictured my daddy. Yes, the man had the same blond hair and attractive smile. They both had nice teeth. Momma Rose thanked God often that Daisy and I were graced with the Richards teeth. However there were some differences. Daddy was tall and lean to the point of being skinny. Whereas the stranger was shorter and stocky. A thought hit me. I looked at Daisy.

"How do you know what Daddy looks like?"

"I saw a picture of him."

"Liar, Momma burned all of Daddy's pictures years ago."

Daisy ran her hand down the doll's hair. Her words soft and unsure. "I saw the one you have tucked away in your bible."

Anger and agitation appeared out of nowhere. Along with the question that sprang from my lips.

"How do you know about the picture in my bible?"

Daisy clammed up.

How did she even know where I kept it hidden? It's not like it was as big as the family bible Momma Rose set out on the coffee table when she thought company might drop in. My bible was white and pocket-sized. Daddy had sent it to me for my seventh birthday. I still remembered how excited and grown up I felt when I came home from school to find the small brown paper box waiting for me.

At eleven I possessed two treasures and Daisy had tarnished them both. My little white bible and one picture of my daddy. Kind of sad when you think about it but it is what it is. I consider myself lucky to have that one picture.

Momma Rose destroyed all traces of my daddy one drunken night. It happened one night, hours after Daisy and I had been sent off to bed. I woke up to the smell of smoke. Thinking the house was on fire I jumped out of the bed and went to the living room.

What I found was Momma Rose sitting in the center of the sofa that stuck us in the butt because of a broken spring. If it was sticking her, Momma Rose didn't show it. In front of her on the coffee table, right beside that family bible I was telling you about, was a tin bucket we used as a trash can. A yellow glow told me that was the source of the smoke though the flame wasn't high enough for me to see it.

Momma Rose drank a dark liquid. I knew that it could not be soda. Momma hated the stuff and refused to buy it for us. Thelma told me and Daisy that Momma had a "stash" of alcohol that she kept hidden in her room. She claimed that Momma Rose drank after we went to bed and witnessing this, I guessed Thelma to be right.

But I'm getting off point. Momma would take a drink then throw a picture on the fire. I stood there and watched. I doubt she ever knew I was there. The hall was off to the side and out of her direct line of vision. I waited and watched. Both sad and angry. Sad that Momma Rose seemed upset and angry that she took away the only connection I had to my daddy. When she finally finished, Momma Rose stared at the fire until it burned itself out. Then she pulled down the handmade afghan from the back of the sofa and curled up into a ball.

Realizing the show was over I turned to go back to bed. That's when I saw it. Momma Rose missed one. She missed a picture that had slipped underneath the table. I tip-toed over to the table, careful not to make a peep, and retrieved the treasure. It was a picture of my daddy from the war. He stood on a dirt road holding up a crudely made sign that simply said "I love you."

That picture was the one link to my daddy. I forgot his voice after about a year and I was determined to never forget what he looked like. When I grew sad or lonely I would take the picture out and pretend that Daddy was holding that sign up for me. Telling me he loved me.

I realized that Daisy had been watching me. Waiting for me to respond or better yet for me to yell at her. Not one to disappoint I did just that. "What did I tell you about snooping through my stuff?"

"I wasn't snooping this time. Honestly, May, I wasn't. I wanted something to read."

"You ask people before you go through their stuff. You hear me?"

Daisy nodded but it's not like she listened. I could have went one but just did not feel like it. The next time we would have the same conversation again. We rarely ever fought. Mostly we bickered but when it did happen it never stopped until an adult got involved. If it was Momma Rose (and it normally was) she would begin screaming at us both. By the time we were sent to our room the only thing we could talk about was what in the hell was wrong with Momma? Our argument with each other long forgotten.

* * *

A screen slamming back on its squeaky hinges drew our attention to the house next door. An older man stepped off the back stoop. Unlike our house, there was no porch to shade from the sunlight. I watched as the man lifted a coffee cup to his lips. His lips tightened into a hard line, making me think the brew may be bitter. My observation proved right when a minute later he poured the liquid into a nearby rosebush.

Daisy slipped off the swing and began playing with her doll on the ground. Her interest in the old man clearly waning even if mine had not. I watched him. His hair, what he had of it, was brown. Not light or dark, just brown. He wore a pair of black-rimmed glasses. His clothing of a short sleeve white button up shirt and black slacks were simple but well made.

If you were to ask me I would have told you he looked like a Grandpa. Not that I would know. Momma Rose's daddy died before I was born and my daddy's dad, well you know about that. I do not know a thing about Daddy's people. They may all be dead or they may all be alive. The second thought bothered me more than the first. If they were dead they couldn't come to visit me and Daisy. But if they were alive they chose not know me.

"Who are you staring at girl?"

I had been busted and almost jumped out of my skin. Lost in my own thought I failed to see the old man looking back at me. I immediately jumped to my feet and senseless words tumbled from my lips.

"Well…I…No…I mean…I'm not."

"It sure looks like you were eyeballing me."

"I wasn't. I promise."

"What's your name?" the sharp edge was now softer. His voice remained gruff but I reckon that came from a lifetime of living and not me staring at him.

"May Reynolds."

He nodded and proceeded to walk over to the chain link fence that separated the two properties. "Vera said something about new people moving in."

I didn't know who Vera was but I nodded.

He held out his hand. "The name's Jesse but you can call me J.D. Everyone else does."

I looked at his hand. I had never shook anyone's hand before. That was something adults did. Not wanting to make him mad, I put my small hand in his much larger one. "J.D."

He gave my hand a light squeeze and then let go. "What's your daddy do?"

That was a question I had been asked time and time again. I use to struggle with an answer until I told Momma Rose about it. Now I had my reply down pat. "It's just Momma and us girls."

J.D. nodded like he understood. "So it's you, your mother, and—?" He pointed toward Daisy.

"That's my sister Daisy and my cousin Thelma also stays with us."

"Four women and one bathroom? I bet that's hell trying to go anywhere," he chuckled.

I smiled.

"Where's your Mother now?"

"She's done gone to see our old landlord about getting the deposit back."

Before either of us could say anything else there was a noise from inside. After hearing it a second time, I comprehended it to be a voice. A male voice. I prayed it wasn't Vera. "Grandpa?"

J.D.'s face softened into a grin. "Out here, son."

I heard something heavy hit the ground. I listened so intently that I swore I heard footfalls across the linoleum tiles. One glance at J.D. and I could see he was listening as well.

I know at eleven I had not seen every man in the world but as the door opened I knew this tall, lanky boy was something special. I guessed him to be about Thelma's age. He was dressed in a navy suit without a tie. The top button was undone and he had flipped the collar up against his neck. His brown hair was slicked back in and he had the longest sideburns I had ever seen.

J.D. moved away from the fence. I took the few moments he forgot I was there to be a spectator. Watching them like I did everything else. Like I was watching a movie or television show. The boy, whose eyes were the most amazing shade of blue (I could see them even at this distance) focused on J.D. I doubt he even saw me.

"Vera told me you would come," J.D. said, stopping in from of the younger man.

"Yes sir," the boy answered politely.

"I didn't think your mother would let you. I thought after what happened…"

"Think nothing of it."

I did not have a clue what they were talking about but I could call bull when I heard it. Whatever had happened, this boy thought of it and thought of it often if my intuition was right. They stood there watching each other. Neither seemed to know what to do next.

It saddened me and maybe that was why I ran over to the fence and exclaimed, "Hi! I'm May and that over there is my sister Daisy."

The boy's eyes flew to mine immediately. I was right. He had not seen me before.

J.D. stepped back. "I almost forgot my new friend here. Her family moved in today. May, I would like you to meet my grandson, Elvis."

"What kind of name is Elvis?" Daisy blurted out. So she had been listening.

"The one my mother gave me," he said, taking affront. His jaw tightened. As quickly as he answered I bet he had been asked the question before. Asked as carelessly as people asked about my daddy.

"She didn't mean anything by it," I said, trying to make things better. "It's just unusual is all."

Was that any better? I wanted to crawl into a hole.

The boy named Elvis did not seem to care though. He spoke to J.D.

"If you don't mind, sir, it was a mighty long bus ride and I would like to go inside."

"I'll show you the room Vera set up for you," J.D. said as Elvis held the door open for his grandfather to go inside. "It's not much, but I think you will like the place."

Before walking inside, Elvis glanced over his shoulder at me. I was sure he didn't like me. What was there to like? He thought I was funning him.

"Unusual, huh?"

I nodded for it was an unusual name and I refused to say otherwise. Even if the boy with the beautiful eyes hated me. But Elvis didn't hate me. He smiled.

"I like that," and then he disappeared into the house.

# CHAPTER FOUR

It took all of two days for Thelma to find out about Elvis. That night, as Momma Rose fixed dinner and Daisy and I set the table, she came flouncing in and plopped herself down into a kitchen chair.

"I met a boy today."

"Why am I not surprised?" Momma Rose asked.

Thelma sat up and spoke to me. "He's visiting next door. A total dreamboat."

"Well does Mr. Dreamboat have a name?"

"Elvis."

"Elvis?" Momma Rose snorted, "What kind of name is that?"

"The kind his momma gave him," I parroted his response from our meeting.

Thelma reached out and tucked a strand of hair behind my ear. "Aunt Rose, May needs a haircut. It's getting in her face again."

"Tell me about Elvis," I said, cleverly changing the subject back before Momma Rose went on and on about the price of going to the hair salon. Then she would say she might as well cut my hair herself. I still had not fully recovered from the last scalping she gave me the previous winter.

Thelma, completely enthralled with her new "friend," was more than happy to oblige. "I met him this morning on my way to the library."

I left that lie alone. She told Momma Rose about the library when in fact she was meeting a bunch of her friends for an impromptu party at an abandoned house. I figured what Momma did not know kept us all out of trouble.

"He was cutting the grass. I knew that he saw me as I made my way down the sidewalk because he stopped and pulled a handkerchief out of his pocket. He wiped his brow and put the handkerchief away before speaking to me."

"Then how do you know he saw you?" Daisy asked, "Maybe he was just sweaty."

"Trust me Daisy, he saw me and he liked what he saw."

"Girl," Momma Rose said, turning off the stove, "you are too horny for your own good."

Now I would be sixteen before I would know the exact definition of horny. Knowing Thelma though, I had a pretty accurate understanding of the word at eleven. Thelma's cheeks burned a bright red but went on talking.

"He has such polite manners. He said he's up here for the summer visiting his grandfather."

"That's nice," Momma Rose said, looking at me, "Bring me your sister's bowl."

"Why can't Daisy do it?" I whined. Being the older sister was not all it was cracked up to be when Momma treated Daisy like a baby.

"Because Daisy would spill half the bowl before she got it to the table. Do you want to give her your share of dinner or bring me her bowl?"

This week we barely had enough food to fill out bellies. Momma Rose got paid every two weeks and ones she did not get paid were lean. I got to my feet. I sure wasn't going to go without just because I was lazy. I could not miss the little smirk on Momma's face as she took the bowl from me. She usually got her way. I hoped that she would one day teach me her tricks.

"Not beans again," Thelma moaned, "Don't you get tired of the same thing every day?"

Daisy and I knew not to answer. Dinner on most night consisted of little more than beans and taters. It was an inexpensive meal Momma Rose was especially good at cooking. But to say that wouldn't make Thelma like us any better. Momma Rose and Thelma were keen to our survival. Neither was a wanted enemy. Momma Rose fed, sheltered, clothed us, and supplied the occasional goodies. Thelma acted as the cool older cousin who told dirty jokes and told about the things Momma thought we were too young to know about.

Momma Rose took a seat at the table. "I like beans and taters. Let me tell you what I do get tired of—"

"That mouth!" Daisy, Thelma, and I chimed in unison. That threw us girls into a fit of giggles and earned a smile from Momma Rose.

"That's right. May say grace."

I hated saying grace. Not because I hated God or am mad at him. I just hated all the attention and pressure it brought with it. I never knew what to say and it all came out sounding stupid. It was the rule that we all took turns. Momma Rose was the best at it. Thelma's always the same "Thank you for this food and our family. Amen."

Daisy's usually sounded more like a nighttime prayer. She started with thank you for this food and ended several minutes later with her seemingly endless list of what I called the God Blesses. Many a night as Daisy went on and our bellies began to rumble I thought of stopping her. A sharp look from Momma Rose put a quick end to the idea. Once Daisy finished, Momma would tell her that the blessing was perfect.

"Thank you, Lord, for this nutritious meal that Momma Rose made us. Amen."

It must have been good enough for there were a round of amens and then we began to eat.

"I thought you were still dating Eddie," Momma Rose said after a few minutes.

"I am."

"Then if Eddie is so wonderful why are you sniffing around this other boy?"

Thelma shrugged her shoulders. "Eddie doesn't own me. Besides, Elvis is only here for the summer."

Momma held her fork to her lips. She looked from Thelma and then down at her plate. "You need to keep that in mind, girl. Don't go getting your heart broken."

"I won't, I promise."

I hated the turn the conversation was taking. Talking about Elvis as if he already belonged to Thelma did not seem fair. I mean I know an eleven year old girl had no hope romantically with a boy Elvis's age, but I met him first. I bit my tongue to keep myself from calling dibs.

"What else did he say?" I asked.

"Not much. He said that he could play the guitar and sing a little bit. Not that it impressed me. I mean, Eddie can play the guitar."

"And we all know what a genius he is," Momma said.

I smiled at Momma's joke and she looked at me a bit strangely. Like she was reading my mind and didn't like what she saw. I wished I wasn't so jealous. I loved it when Momma teased. Always quick-witted, Momma Rose said lots of funny things. But often they were without her smile and seemed hard, sarcastic, and at times downright mean. This was not one of those times. This time was a joke.

"Anyway, his grandpa came outside and began griping about the yard not being done. So we said goodbye and I went to the library."

"You planning on seeing him again?" I could not help myself.

"Of course silly, he's staying right next door. If he's lucky, I'll let him see me."

My stomach dropped. I kept eating but the soup beans might as well have been water for all I could taste them. Thelma was like a baby with a new toy. Once the newness of Elvis wore off she will move on to the next boy. It just didn't seem fair. I liked Elvis. Maybe it was because like Thelma, I thought him new and interesting. In a day or two I would move on as well. I hoped I did any way.

As dinner went on I tried not to notice Momma Rose keeping an eye on me. Daisy and Thelma were the big talkers. I had no problem sitting and listening to their stories. In fact, I preferred it. Even at my tender age I knew we could not all be larger than life personalities. I heard someone once say we can't all be princesses. For who would clap when we passed by? I knew that I was the one clapping.

So me not talking much was nothing new. Momma Rose watching me, now that was different. I plastered a fool's grin on my face. I offered up questions, advice, and laughter to any jokes in hopes of sending Momma Rose off my scent. By the end of the night I was exhausted and not even positive I succeeded.

\* \* \*

We spent the next week getting the house to rights and falling into a new routine. I was always an early riser. Living in a house as opposed to an apartment allowed me new opportunities. In an apartment building full of strangers, Momma Rose had a rule that Daisy and I couldn't go outside alone. That meant that if I wanted to go outside I had to wait most days until high noon at the earliest because my lazy bones sister did not want to get up.

Now that we had a house to ourselves, Momma Rose said it was okay for us to go out and play alone. Each morning I would get cleaned up, go into the kitchen for a glass of lemonade, and then head out to the porch swing. Most days I brought a book that I had borrowed from the library or my little bible. I tried to understand the bible but most of it was just words. You know, so and so begat so and so and what not. I tried to ask Momma Rose about it but she didn't know any more than I did. But I figured God gave me credit for trying.

On the third morning, J.D. was sitting at the picnic table. He wore a blue work suit that was unbuttoned to show a white undershirt. Thelma heard from Elvis that J.D. worked nights at Pepsi Bottling Company as a watchman. It was startling to have someone break my silence and I almost returned to the house in hopes that he would soon be gone.

"Morning," J.D. called out to me, lifting the blue and white coffee cup to his lips.

"Good morning," I called back, sounding a lot more chipper than I felt.

He motioned toward the swing. "Don't let me being out here keep you from your routine. I'll be headed off to bed soon enough."

And that was how we began. From that morning on, J.D. and I would share that twilight hour before my world awoke and his went to dreamland. We did not talk. We didn't have to. Instead I would read my book and he flipped through his newspaper. When he finished, he would stand up and stretch. Tucking the paper under his arm, he gave me a nod before heading into the house.

I would always smile and return to my reading. It was nice. Actually it was quite nice. Together but alone. Most people do not understand that, but J.D. did. Or I assumed he did. We did that every day for two weeks. Even on the weekends (I found out were his off days) J.D. showed up.

You can imagine my surprise when on that second Sunday I went outside to no J.D. I tried to not let it bother me. I drank all of my lemonade and read three chapter on my latest book while waiting. After an hour I gave up. I closed my book and looked toward the house. Momma Rose and the girls would be up soon. Then I looked at the house next door.

If I knew them better and was not such a shy person I might have went up and knocked on the screen. Momma Rose said that people hated busybodies and their privacy invaded. But what if something was wrong with J.D.? The two sides tore at me. Wanting to go check and fearing what would happen if I did.

The fear won out and I got to my feet as I heard a screen door. Thinking it was J.D., I started to tease him about being so late. "Well it's about…"

The words died on my lips. You see it wasn't J.D. It was Elvis.

"Morning," he mumbled, glancing a bit nervously over his shoulder.

"Hey," I answered, "where's J.D.?"

Elvis stepped out the back door, pulling the door gently closed behind him. "He's not feeling too good this morning."

"Oh, I hope it's nothing serious," I repeated the words Momma Rose had said dozens of times.

"He'll be fine in a day or so."

I watched Elvis climb up and take a seat on the picnic table. He used the bench as a foot rest. "Can I ask you something?"

I walked over to the fence. We were separated by a few feet. "I guess. Depends on what you are asking."

"Why do you do it?"

"Do what?" For I had no clue what he was talking about.

He motioned for the swing. "This? I've been watching you and my grandpa. How every morning you come out here and sit. Neither one of you saying a thing. Why?"

I wish I could explain it but how could I when I didn't completely understand it myself? I shrugged. "I like him."

"You shouldn't. I don't."

Elvis had opened the subject so Momma Rose's lessons on privacy were void now. "Why not?"

Elvis looked away. "I just don't."

That was no answer and I knew he wanted to tell me.

"Maybe I like him because I don't have a grandpa."

"You don't?" he asked.

"Nope." I shook my head. "I ain't got no daddy neither. Not really. Since he's gone I don't have his daddy and Momma Rose's daddy died before I was born. Come to think of it, I don't have any grandmas either."

"I guess you think I'm wrong."

I shook my head. "You can think whatever you want. I just think you're sad. Don't you like it here?"

His hands were tightly clasped between his bent knees and there was a slight rocking motion. His next words would be a mix of lie and truth. "I like it well enough. I just miss my momma and Dodger."

"Is that your dog?"

A genuine smile played at the corners of his mouth. "Dodger's my grandmother."

"Why call her Dodger? Does she like baseball or something?" I asked. It seemed only logical considering there was a Brooklyn baseball team by the name.

"No, but I like the way you think, pet. When I was a little boy I got mad and threw a baseball at her head. She dodged it and I've been calling her Dodger ever since."

He still rocked slightly but not as much as before. "My daddy thought it would be good for me to come up here this summer. Not that I really get it. He and J.D. never got along. Maybe I'm just one less mouth to feed."

"What did your mother think about you coming here?"

The rocking was back. Clearly I had hit a sore spot. He stared down at the ground. "She hates it. They got into an awful row one night. Next day, they tell me I'm visiting."

Elvis broke my heart with the grief he was feeling. I wanted to reach out and do something. Do anything to help make him feel better. So I shared the only thing I could think of that might help him feel less alone.

"I miss my daddy too."

"Where is he?"

I shrugged. "Momma Rose says he's with his people in Ohio."

"What happened?"

"Momma Rose says some people just aren't meant to be married. I don't believe that. I think she got tired of Daddy not working," I paused for Elvis to agree with me but he didn't and I went on, "They fought all the time about money and when he was going to get a job. So the way I look at it that has to be it."

"That's sounds about right. Money's always been tight with my folks as well. One day I'm going to make enough money so my momma don't ever have to worry about things again."

That was a nice thought. Fixing it so that Momma Rose didn't have to work so hard. It made me feel good to think that one day she might be able to sit back and kick her heels up.

"Me, too, though I don't know how," I said.

"I think I do," he said.

I leaned a little closer to the fence. The sun, still low in the eastern sky, had not warmed the metal post, so I rested my hand on it. I looked at Elvis and he waited to make eye contact. When those blue eyes met mine I knew he believed with his entire soul the words he was about to impart.

"I'm going to be a famous singer."

Thelma would have laughed. Momma would have spouted a sarcastic comment. I did not do either of those things. I believed him. With the look he had on his face, I would have believed him if he had told me he was going to fly to the moon. I only had one question for him.

"How?"

The insecure boy thought I was going to laugh at his idea. It kind of stung that he did not trust me yet. I know that we'd only known each other a few weeks but it felt longer. Especially with his conversations with Thelma that I heard secondhand.

"You can tell me," I nudged him.

A loud bang came from the house, causing Elvis to nervously jump to his feet. He viewed the door and then looked back at me. "I've got to go."

"But—" I said.

"Where the hell are you, boy?" J.D. bellowed from inside the house.

"Not now," Elvis said, "You meet me here tonight. After everyone else is asleep."

He ran back into the house before I could say anything else. As I gathered up my things I heard rumblings from inside and Thelma's voice. Maybe it was better that we waited. If Thelma realized that Elvis was outside talking to me there would have been no stopping her. Maybe even finagling a date with him tonight and then where would I be? Momma Rose didn't raise no fool. An eleven year old girl was no match for Thelma's double Ds when a teenage boy was involved.

## CHAPTER FIVE

By that afternoon I thought I might go crazy thinking about my rendezvous with Elvis. I was daydreaming on my freshly made bed when thankfully Thelma came to my rescue. Momma Rose was no more out the door to go to work when Thelma appeared in the hallway outside my bedroom door. Daisy sat at our plastic kiddie table coloring her latest masterpiece.

"What do you girls want to do today?" Thelma asked. She was wearing her worn crimson bathrobe that she swore made her feel like a movie star.

Daisy and I exchanged a look. She shrugged. "We could listen to the radio."

"Boring," Thelma said, "What about you May? What do you want to do?"

Since "make it nighttime" wasn't a viable answer I went with the typical. "I don't know."

"You girls, I swear I don't know what I'm going to do with you. Where is your sense of adventure?"

"Aren't you going somewhere with Eddie?"

Thelma grinned like she was keeping a secret. "I don't have to see him every day. That would ruin the spark. Besides, he's working and wouldn't like to do this anyway."

I rolled my eyes. "Just tell us already."

"You better stop that before I slap them eyeballs back into place. Keep acting like that and maybe me and Daisy will go without you. It would serve you right."

"Where are we going?" Daisy asked.

Thelma, the dramatic actress, untied her robe and let it fall to her feet. Underneath she wore a red two-piece bathing suit with little black polka dots on it. "We're going to the public pool."

Saying pool to children in the summer came in only second to the melody that played when the ice cream man came barreling down the street. Daisy and I both jumped to our feet. We clasped hands and began jumping around the room chanting "We're going to the pool." Daisy grabbed Thelma's hand and for a couple of choruses even our cool cousin joined the festivities. Afterward we collapsed into a heap of giggles. It wasn't until after we caught out breath that the reality of what Thelma said hit me.

"Did Momma Rose say it was okay?"

"She didn't say it wasn't," Thelma said somewhat sheepishly.

"Did you ask her?" I asked, sounding more like the older cousin.

"May, she would have just been a buzzkill."

Which meant no, Thelma had not asked her.

"Besides, Aunt Rose is completely wrong about swimming. She thinks just because she about drowned a million years ago she's an authority on it."

"Well wouldn't she be? I mean, she does know the danger."

Thelma would not be swayed by my weak argument. "No, she never learned how to swim. I taught you last summer remember? And Daisy can stay in the kiddie pool."

"Hey, I'm not a baby."

Thelma put an arm around Daisy's shoulder. "We know that, sweetie. It's a name for a little pool. I'm willing to bet that there will be a lot of kids there your age. Maybe even a few that will go to your school next year."

Daisy changed her attitude. Her eyes begging me as she knew I was the only holdout. "Please May. I'll love you forever."

"If Momma Rose found out—"

"She won't," Thelma said.

"But if she does..." I trailed off.

"And I'm telling you she won't. Who is going to tell her? None of her old friends live near here and she ain't had the time to make new ones. Come on May...live a little."

Defying Momma Rose, which is what we were doing, was huge. If she found out there was no telling what she would do. Ground us for sure. Yelling? Definitely. If angry enough she might even send Thelma back to her folks. She sure did threaten that enough. I hated the thought of testing Momma's love for Thelma against her fear of the water. The winner was unclear and I liked to bet on a sure thing.

Seeing that I was on the verge of saying no she pulled out the only ace she had left. "I'll let you wear one of my old suits."

That did it. "The yellow one with the ruffles?"

Thelma nodded. "We will have to pin it up a little for you. And I will even put a little rouge and lipstick on you for all the boys to admire."

We were off and running an hour later.

* * *

Now when Thelma said that we were going to the pool, I assumed that she had the money for all three admissions plus the bus fare. I was wrong. We trekked four miles in the sun. I thought poor Daisy might faint after the third time we stopped for her to rest. Then when we got there, Thelma left us outside the gate. She told us to wait and that she would come and get us as soon as possible.

Daisy and I watched as she flirted with a big, beefy looking lifeguard for a while. We watched as kid after kid paid their quarter and went inside. From our post I could see the mountainous diving board. One after another made the long climb up the ladder and jumped off. As laughter rang out all around us I grew angry. The longer we waited, the more Daisy's shoulders began to slump. A few of the nicer women arriving with children in tow asked if we were okay. Daisy did not speak to them. She kept her attention on the pool. I tried to smile and explained that we were waiting on our cousin.

Finally she looked up at me. A small hand shading her eyes. "We aren't going in there, are we?"

"I don't know. Thelma wouldn't have brought us here if she didn't think she could," I said.

"Why would she bring us here if she didn't have the money? Momma Rose wouldn't have."

Another question I couldn't answer. So I said nothing.

"I wish I had two quarters," Daisy sighed.

Every poor kid has that moment. The one where they realize that they are poor. Mine came when I could not go on a school trip to the zoo. Daddy had left us not long before and spare money didn't grow on trees. This was Daisy's moment and I knew exactly how it felt. I longed to take that feeling away.

"I wish I had one quarter so you could go in."

Daisy shook her head. "It wouldn't be any fun without you."

"You know what?" I asked as I took her towel and put it under my arm.

"What?"

"I bet the water hose at the house will be just as cold as that water there and we wouldn't have to share it with anyone. I bet we'd have just as much fun."

Daisy knew I lied, but bless her heart, she went along with it. "I bet you're right. What about Thelma?"

"It would serve her right if we left. Can you imagine how scared she would get if she found us gone? Maybe we ought to stay away until Momma Rose gets home from work. That would teach Thelma a lesson."

"And get us a whooping."

"True."

I learned from the several whoopings I earned over the years that I could go my whole life without getting another one. Especially when Momma Rose was mad and she was never madder than when she was scared. My idea, while good in theory, would be lousy in action. I took Daisy's hand.

The pool was fenced in with a long concrete building that backed up to a wooded area. I figured that if we walked along the line we could get Thelma's attention.

"Let's go."

\* \* \*

Fallen tree branches crunching under my feet made me grateful for wearing my white sneakers instead of sandals. Daisy, however, chose the sandals and forced us to stop every few yards to remove a twig or rock. It hampered our pace and stretched my already fraying nerves.

The building was longer than I imagined or maybe it was all the stops we made. By the time we got to the corner of the building we had to stop again. That was when I heard voices. I placed a finger to my lips to shush Daisy and lifted a low lying branch that blocked my view. At the edge of the building where it met the fence we saw a group of kids standing in a line. A blond-haired boy in dirty jeans and a dingy white t-shirt was holding back the metal chain link. A portly boy about ten placed something shiny in the dirty boy's hand. It looked silver. A dime, maybe?

"Now," the older boy whispered, his tone denouncing the urgency. Crawling through the opening the portly boy lumbered to his feet on the other side and walked away without a backward glance. I glanced to the lifeguard stand. Thelma still had the young man's attention. He had no idea how many people were there. Free, reduced, or fully paid.

"What are they doing?" Daisy whispered to me.

"Shh, that boy's sneaking them in."

Another kid, this time a girl of about fourteen, paid the fare and went inside.

"But if they have the money why don't they go in the gate?"

"Because they don't have enough."

The last kid, an acne-faced boy, slipped inside. The blond securely placed the fencing back in place so that no one would notice something was amiss. He stood up and patted his pocket. From the sound of the slight jingle I heard I'd bet he had at least five dollars' worth of change. Apparently smuggling was a good business.

He was tall and lean to the point of almost being skinny. There was a hungry look to him. Like he could use more than a few home cooked meals. His back straightened when he saw us.

"What are you looking at?" he asked, put out, "Pool's closed. No one else today."

"What?" I asked, trying to gather the wool from my thoughts. You know how when you looked into the sky on a sunny day you get a little dazed. That was how I felt after looking into this boy's blue green eyes, "We don't want in. We were just going home."

I saw that he didn't believe me. He put his back up against the building and pulled a cigarette out of his back pocket. Out of his front pocket he produced matches. One strike and he lit the cigarette and then shook out the flame.

"Then what are you doing back here?"

"We need to tell our cousin we're going home," Daisy offered up.

Eyeing me he turned to Daisy. "Why didn't you tell her before you left?"

"Oh, we didn't have the money to go inside," Daisy said to my mortification.

He took a drag off the cigarette before dropping it to the ground and rubbing it out with his foot. "You didn't see what went on here. You got me?"

I know he meant to scare us but it was hard to take him seriously. I mean, he was movie star handsome. My heart gave a little skip and began to beat faster. What was wrong with me? Was I coming down with the flu?

"I've got a sweet deal going on here and I won't have it ruined by a pair of goody two shoes."

"I'm not a goody two shoes," I said.

He stepped closer. The menacing look would have worked if he had not been so good looking. As it was I just wanted to hug him close and maybe, if I was being honest, kiss him like I saw in the movies. Like Thelma kissed Eddie when she thought I was tucked away in bed.

"Prove it."

I rolled my eyes. "I don't have to prove anything to you."

He gave me a cocky grin before bending down to talk to Daisy. The grin grew into a genuine smile.

"What's your name, sweetheart?"

"Daisy. And this is my sister May."

"May, huh," he said, seeming to try the name out on his lips before shooting his eyes up to mine, "the name's Jack Dewitt."

Jack. I liked it. In all honestly though he could have introduced himself as KoKo the clown and I would have thought it the dreamiest name in the world.

"Tell you what Daisy. How about I give you a freebie this time."

"What do you think May?" Daisy asked.

"We don't need any help."

Jack stood back up. Even skinny he was still a head taller than me. "Did I say anything about helping you?"

"Then why let her in and not me?"

"Because I like her."

There had to be a catch. Just like Thelma this morning who had no money but was convinced in her wiles that she could get us inside. I could hear Momma Rose's voice telling me that nothing in this life was free.

"Come on Daisy," I said, pushing my way past Jack like I was the Queen of Sheba wrapped in a royal robe instead of two discolored towel clutched to my chest. This whole day was getting ridiculous. Going home, eating lunch, and thinking about my meeting with Elvis was all I wanted. Maybe that would get Jack and his smile out of my head.

When I got to the fence I saw Thelma. She seemed to be looking around between flirts. I figured she finally noticed we were not where she left us. I started to call out for her when something clamped down on my mouth. It took half a second to realize it was Jack's hand.

He pulled me back out of sight. "Are you crazy?"

As he was letting me go Daisy got in one good kick to Jack's shin.

"Now why did you have to go and do that you little ankle biter? I wasn't going to hurt her." Jack rubbed his injured limb. "I just didn't want you to ruin my business."

"I wasn't going to ruin your business. I was just going to talk to Thelma."

Jack took a deep breath and ran his fingers through his hair. "I need this money all right? You call out to your cousin and she brings that gorilla in a swimsuit, I'm done for."

"He wouldn't know it was you."

"I've kind of got a reputation around here."

"You could always go to another pool," Daisy offered, trying to be helpful.

"The closest pool is about three miles that way. Churchill Country Club."

"That's not too far," I said.

"They've got three foot stone walls. Hard to cut a hole in if you know what I mean."

Well he had me there. "Okay, but I still need to talk to my cousin."

"I can let her in," Jack said, not bothering to wait for my agreement. Instead he went back to the fence and just as effortlessly pulled back and produced the entry way. He motioned to Daisy. She walked over and bent down beside him. Apparently she had made an executive decision on the matter. With a whisper in her ear, Daisy nodded.

"Now," he said.

Daisy moved faster than I had ever seen her. Once on the other side she jumped to her feet and made a beeline for Thelma who sighed in relief upon seeing her youngest charge.

With Daisy in the clear, Jack put everything to right.

"What about me?" I asked, feeling stupid.

"Daisy's enough. I told her to tell your cousin that you would meet them outside the gate in fifteen minutes. I can't have you both appearing out of the clear blue."

"And why not? Thelma knows I would never leave Daisy alone."

"Can't take the chance," Jack placed his hands in his pockets. I heard the coins jingle.

"How much do you charge them?"

"Not much. Just a dime," Jack went back behind the building. I knew it was because he feared being caught.

I followed him. "And people pay you?"

"Yep."

"Why? Anyone could cut a hole and run in."

"True, but no one knows this place like me. I know the pool and the people. I picked this part not only because it's difficult to see from the lifeguard post but it's also highly travelled by people going to the bathroom and refreshment stand. I get paid to know how to safely sneak in. I get paid for that and to take the blame if we are caught."

"That seems like a pretty big risk for a dime."

"A dime per person. You've got to remember that. Minimum wage is what? Seventy five cents an hour? If I worked eight hours pumping gas and cleaning windshields at the end of the day I would make six bucks. Hell, I do half the work and make five in two or three hours on good days. Plus I don't answer to no boss man who thinks he's better than me."

"How old are you?" I asked, disbelieving such a young boy could do that kind of math and reasoning.

Jack smiled. "I just turned thirteen last week. How old are you?"

I did the only thing a girl could do when a male asked her age. I lied. Besides it was a white lie. I would be twelve at the beginning of the month. I figured what Jack didn't know wouldn't hurt him. "Twelve."

"You look older. I thought you were at least fourteen."

That brightened my day. "I wish."

"I know what you mean. One day closer to leaving this Godforsaken town," he said, mistaking my meaning.

"I guess so," I said, not dispelling his belief. Never had I given much thought about leaving Louisville. It was where I was born. Where I was raised. Where my family lived. I figured that I would live with Momma Rose until after high school or longer. Then I might get a job as a sales girl or secretary in some office before getting married and having babies.

"Why do you want to leave?" I asked.

I watched his jaw tighten and release. "No reason. Just the usual stuff. Parents, school, you know."

"Where would you go?"

When he spoke there was no hesitation or vagueness to his answer.

"Anywhere I wanted. One of my brothers saw New York City when he was in the Navy. He didn't like it none. Said it was too loud for him. But I think I would like it. I'm thinking there or out West?"

"And be a cowboy?" I teased, moving to stand beside him.

He looked down and laughed. "No, Miss smartie."

"What's out there?"

"A lot of things. California for one. That would be nice. Sun, sand, beautiful people, what's not to love?" When he put it that way it did not sound half bad. "Hollywood is out there too. Maybe I could be an actor."

"Is that what you want to do?"

"Don't know," he shrugged, "what I do know is that I want to be out of here. For now, that's enough."

I bit my lip. "Is that why you do this?"

"No. My old man lost his job about a year ago. He picks up odd jobs when he can. We need the money so I do what I have to do."

"Does he know what you do?" I turned against the building and propped myself up on my shoulder. Jack studied me but didn't move. I heard the change rattle again. It must be a nervous tick.

"He could care less how I pick up a few bucks. It's just important that I do."

Worry beyond his years were etched in Jack's face. Just like Momma Rose. He looked as if life had taken a toll on him. I waited for him to go on but he didn't for a long time. Then eventually he grew uncomfortable enough that he finally spoke.

"What are you looking at?"

"I like you, Jack Dewitt," I said, smiling up at him. The words fell from my lips quickly. Five words, one sentence, never felt so right in all of my life. I did like him.

"You shouldn't."

That was all he said before checking to see that the coast was clear. He walked away, not once peeking over his shoulder. Not a word did he call out. I thought of the Tin Man from the Wizard of Oz. How he knew he had a heart because it was breaking. Mine was not as much broken as it was bruised. My pride hurt more. By the way…I never made it into the pool that day.

* * *

Thelma apologized the entire way home. Of course that was after she boxed my ears for wandering off. I tried to explain but she didn't want to hear it. However, Daisy and I heard all about how hard Thelma worked the lifeguard gorilla (Jack' word for him) to see about getting us in. Unfortunately Thelma's gorilla was smarter than he looked or just not that into her.

Once she realized we were gone from the front gate she said that she knew we wouldn't go far. She said that she continued to work the lifeguard while trying to look for us. I don't know if I completely believe her. I'm sure she was worried and looked some but for how long I sincerely call into question.

Back at the house we all changed clothes. I washed out the swimsuit and hung them out to dry while Daisy (who got to swim) had Thelma wash out her hair in the sink. Lunch consisted of peanut butter and jelly sandwiches and a glass of milk. Sun drained and bellies full each of us collapsed for a midafternoon nap. Thelma on the couch and me in the oversized chair. Poor Daisy, with no other place to lay in the living room, crashed out on the rug in front of the television.

Two hours later and the sun beginning to set in the west, I awoke with a jump. That sometimes happened and I had no clue why. Momma Rose said it was my nerves. That my dreams were so real to me that my nerves got tangled up that was why I woke the way I did.

I quietly got to my feet. Experience told me not wake either my sister or cousin. Let them get up on their own and they were fine. Even happy some days but rouse them out of a sound sleep caused misery for all involved. I tiptoed down the hall. The only sound being the click on the bedroom door as I closed it behind me.

I took a seat at the mirror vanity that was on Thelma's side of the room. She rarely let Daisy or I use it. She didn't want our "grubby little hands" destroying it. I respected Thelma's privacy mainly out of fear, but not today. I sat down on the hard wooden chair and looked at my reflection.

My eyes are definitely my best feature. Momma Rose said I had Daddy's blue eyes. Momma Rose, Daisy, and Thelma all had brown eyes. I felt lucky to be different in that, if nothing else. Staring at the rest of my face I saw nothing special. It was neither too thin nor too fat. My cheeks were full but there was a nice rosy hue to them. I might not be beautiful, but I knew I was not ugly either. So I was left to ponder why Jack reacted the way he did. With that in mind, I drove myself crazy for the next few hours.

# CHAPTER SIX

Momma Rose loved her job at Taylor's. From the people she worked with who she thought of as family to the customers who shared their lives with her. The bad thing about Taylor's was the salary did not support a woman, two little girls, and a wayward niece. That was where the second job came in.

Cleaning office buildings at night paid decent but stole away Momma Rose's happiness. Three to four nights a week she came home from her shift at Taylor's and did three things. First, she changed out of her pressed white Taylor's uniform into more comfortable clothes. Then she fixed supper for us girls. Nothing special, but hot (remember the beans and taters from earlier). Third, she would kiss me and Daisy on the forehead and told Thelma no shenanigans and no boys. Thelma would promise with fingers crossed behind her back and Momma Rose would be off again.

This night was different. Wouldn't you know it? Momma Rose didn't go to her night job. After dinner she turned on the radio and collapsed on the couch. Daisy and I gave each other a befuddled look as we washes the dishes. Momma relaxing was a foreign concept. Especially on days she worked her night job. She usually rushed off so she didn't miss the last bus for the evening.

Thelma, who had plans of her own, finally broke down and asked Momma Rose when she was leaving. Momma didn't say anything for a long, drawn out breath. When she finally spoke, you could have knocked me over with a feather with what she said. Momma Rose had been fired. She didn't go into details, and believe me we tried asking questions. The only thing she did say was that her boss accused her of something and she had told the son of a bitch where to go.

As far as I knew, Momma Rose had never been fired from a job. Never as much been late or called in sick. She was a worker. Idle hands and all that jazz. Seeing her lying motionless on the couch was bewildering. We waited for her to get up and tell us to do something but she didn't. Instead she sat there, listening to Hank Williams on the radio. Hank had died in January on a way to a show. It was a sad day in our house. Momma Rose loved Hank and said he reminded her of Daddy. I thought it strange considering how much she claimed to hate Daddy.

Momma Rose was still on the couch by the time I was supposed to meet Elvis. I shuddered at the thought of what she would say were I to walk through the living room and tell her that I was leaving to talk to a boy. Instead, I told her that I was going to bed. I figured that I would have to sneak out. Thelma was straddling the window sill about ready to duck out for the evening.

"Shut the door," she said quickly.

"Where are you going?" I said, shutting the door and leaning back on it.

"I've got a date. I'll back by morning."

"Be careful," I said, withholding my usual judgment as I planned to do the very same thing. I waited fifteen minutes and listened at the door to make sure Momma Rose was not near the kitchen. I climbed out the window and my adventure was on.

\* \* \*

The moon hid behind the clouds and gave the night an inky feeling. My eyes took a moment to adjust to the darkness. As they did, I shook my unease and convinced myself that I had nothing to be afraid of. Besides, if any goblins or bad guys came around, I was sure that Elvis could handle them. I made my way around the side of the house.

The Presley's porch light was lit, so I saw Elvis before he saw me. He wore a dark suit, navy or black, and a white dress shirt. His hair was slicked back and I smelled aftershave in the air. A lot of aftershave. Suddenly, I felt completely underdressed in my brown short and pink halter top.

"Where are you going?" I asked, coming up to the fence. It was becoming our place.

"I was about to give up on you, pet." He looked up and smiled.

I did not remark on him calling me "pet". "Momma Rose lost one of her jobs today. It was hard getting out of the house with her here."

He nodded like he understood. "So you ready to go?"

"Where are we going? I can't." I glanced over my shoulder toward the house.

"Too many ears here."

"I don't know," I started to say. Momma Rose finding me out in the back yard this time of night would get me in trouble. Finding me elsewhere with an older boy might earn me a well-deserved beating.

"Come on, pet. We'll just walk down the sidewalk or a few blocks. When we're done I'll even walk you back before I head out. No one will have to know."

I debated the issue with myself. Weighing the risk versus the reward. Our street was pretty deserted and Momma Rose thought me safely tucked away in bed. Besides, it was not as if anything would happen. We were just going for walk. Elvis was not a bad man.

*He doesn't even have a mustache*, I told myself, *Villains always have a mustache.*

"I'll meet you out front," I said, hurrying out the gate before I could change my mind.

# CHAPTER SEVEN

We made it three whole blocks before either of us had the nerve to speak. Seeing that I would have to be the brave one, I decided to go first.

"So you want to be a singer."

"I sure do. More than anything."

"Can you sing?" I asked. It was a good question but by way his mouth tightened he hated the question. "My friend Cecily, at my old school, told everyone she could dance and boy was she wrong. At the school talent show no one booed her but they just gave her those short polite claps. You know the ones you give when you don't want to hurt someone's feelings."

"I'm good. I won my talent show," he said with the emphasis on won, "and Momma likes my singing."

"Mothers are supposed to like our singing. I sing like a dying cat and Momma Rose smiles like it the neatest thing she's ever heard."

"She wouldn't lie to me," he said, angry. We walked a bit farther in silence. I knew I bruised his ego but chose to ignore it.

"Let's say you can sing. What are you going to do about it?"

"I'm going to sing. I don't know how or where but I'm going to. There are some jazz and blues clubs back home. I'm thinking of approaching them. Then there is always the Opry."

"The Opry is for country music."

"I know that, but I can also sing gospel."

"Well that might work but it's still not country," I said, thinking about Hank. "Country music is all about love, broken hearts and cheating people."

"I can do that. You need to hear me sing, pet. I ain't like nothing you've ever heard before."

"Is singing all you want to do?"

He looked down at his shoes and added softly, "It's all I've ever wanted."

"Then I think you should go for it," I said, surprising even myself. "Who knows, maybe you can go to Hollywood and become one of those famous singing cowboys."

Elvis laughed. "That's cool and all, but I think Roy Rogers' got that covered already. Besides, that's not my sound."

"What is your sound? If I haven't heard it, maybe it hasn't been invented yet."

"Pet, I think you're right," Elvis paused and looked around, "I should probably get you back home before someone realizes you're gone."

Only then did I realize how far away we had walked in the dark. We turned and started back. "Where are you going tonight?"

"A blues club called the Nightingale."

"Isn't it kind of late to be going now?"

"Pet, places I go don't even get started until midnight or later. Then the music goes until people pass out or the sun shines."

"Whichever comes first?" I said, already knowing the answer.

"Yes, ma'am," he agrees with a grin.

For some unreason other than I just wanted him to Jack Dewitt flashes in my brain. I figured I'd ask Elvis about it. He was a boy. Maybe he could explain it to me.

"Can you answer a question for me?"

"I can try."

I then asked the universal question that has withstood the test of time. "Why are boys stupid?"

This laugh was more than amusement. This one rumbled in his chest. "We aren't stupid, well not all the time. You girls just think you are smarter."

"We are."

It was then that the story of the pool and Jack came out. I told Elvis everything. How I shared my feelings for Jack and he walked away like I didn't even matter. By the time I got to that, we were standing back in front of his house.

"It mattered to him, pet," he said, "if it didn't he wouldn't have run off like that. As it was he didn't know what to say. Boys like girls that they have to chase a little."

"Thelma says it's better to be direct. She says boys like that."

Elvis sighed deeply. "I have no doubt the boys your cousin associates with appreciates her, what's the word I'm looking for? Her openness. But trust me, pet, you don't want their kind of attention."

"Then what should I do if I see him again?"

Elvis shifted from one foot to the other. "Don't tell him you like him again until he says it to you. Other than that just be yourself. If he doesn't like you for who you are then he's not worth your time."

"Thank you."

"No need, pet."

I started to walk away but stopped and looked up at him. "I will see you tomorrow?"

"Now that you know about my music who else would I talk to about it?"

For the second time that day a boy had walked away from me. Only this time I giggled. Elvis had that effect on me. He made me special in a world that did not.

"And tell him your real age before I do," he shouted out as he rounded the corner.

Once Elvis was out of sight I turned to go inside. A car door slammed. The noise came from across the street. The blond-haired man from moving day stood beside his car, staring at me. My heart dropped to my stomach as he made his way to the front and leaned back against the hood.

I stood glued to the spot as if he buried me in concrete. I couldn't move, couldn't breathe, couldn't even think clearly. Would he tell Momma Rose? Other than sneaking out, Elvis and I had done nothing wrong. But the man didn't know that. The man pushed himself off of the car and strolled toward his front door. Once his front door shut, the spell was broken and I ran back to my bed.

I didn't sleep a wink that night.

# CHAPTER EIGHT

For the next couple of days, I admit being a complete witch. Worried that the hammer might drop, I snapped at any little thing that displeased me. Momma Rose commented on my attitude after telling Daisy to shut up at the dinner table. Well, she did not comment on it as much as told me to check myself before she did it for me.

I started to argue that she was one to talk. Her attitude was not much better than mine. She still went to work every morning but when she got home the tired look I was use to wasn't there. She looked worried now. The worried look that told me if things did not change soon that we would likely be on the move again.

I hated that look. Especially now. I liked living here on Haywood. J.D. had returned to our morning ritual on Monday. There was my new friend Elvis and then there was Jack. Not that I had seen Jack in those few days but I knew I could always go see him at the pool. If we moved I might not ever see him again.

None of us brought up moving to Momma Rose. I think we all feared what her answer might mean. Things for us girls were going nicely and none of us wanted it to change. So we waited and pretended that there was no white elephant in the room.

Then Momma Rose walked in one night after work and told us she had a date Friday night. You could have knocked me over with a feather. I could not remember a time that she went on a date. As far as I knew, Daddy was the one and only man Momma Rose ever dated. So you can imagine our excitement when Friday finally arrived.

After arriving home from work, Momma Rose took a quick bath and then got dressed with Thelma, Daisy, and I in attendance. Me and Daisy sat on the bed while Thelma helped Momma. Thelma's real good at hair and by the time they got done, Momma Rose looked like one of those women you see on television.

Momma Rose wore a red dress that had long, tapered sleeves and clung in all the right places. She bought the dress at a yard sale when she and Daddy were married but had never found an occasion to wear it. Year after year it hung in her closet. Now though, she looked beautiful. The dress clearly made for her.

Looking pretty did little to ease her nerves though two glasses of cheap wine Uncle Sonny and Aunt June brought over after we moved in did help. And don't bother pointing out the May/June connection. I get it. But back to Momma. Thelma teased that she was going to get tipsy before she left the house. Momma Rose told her that was the point.

Now all week Momma Rose had been tight-lipped about her date. Thelma guessed that it was her boss at Taylor's. I thought it might be another customer like Daddy and Daisy didn't care. Momma had a date. At different times we all voiced our guesses but she neither confirmed nor denied. Momma Rose was weird like that. I think that she feared the man would cancel if she gave a name. That, or she didn't tell us because if he did cancel we would know that he did the next time we saw him.

When the hour was upon us and the knock on the door came you can imagine the mad dash we made toward the door. Thelma, who had the longest legs, got there first. She pushed me backward.

"Will you two ankle biters stop? It would make Aunt Rose look bad to appear too anxious. Just be cool."

Thelma waited for another knock before she opened the door.

Standing there looking very handsome in his blue print oxford shirt and tan slacks was our blond-haired neighbor across the street. In his hands was a bouquet of wildflowers. I could not concentrate on the picture he made. Only one thought ran through my head. This was the man Momma was going out with? Of course it was my luck. The one neighbor who had seen me out with Elvis was going to date my mother. I immediately felt sick to my stomach. Thankfully, us girls had not ate dinner yet.

I glanced over at Thelma. With her big, dumb smile, she was as shocked as me. Only Daisy seemed unfazed by the situation.

"Good evening, ladies," he said, since none of us had the good sense to talk.

"Good evening," Daisy said. "You live across the street."

"I sure do," he agreed, then talking to Thelma, "Is Rose ready?"

That pulled Thelma out of her shock. She motioned for him to come in and closed the door behind him. "I'm sorry. Come on in, Aunt Rose will be out in a minute."

"Good," he said, stepping inside, "I don't think that we've been properly introduced. I'm Nick. Nick Harris."

"I'm Daisy and this is my sister May," she pointed toward Thelma, "and that's Thelma."

"I know. Your mother has told me a lot about you girls."

*That made one of us*, I thought to myself but knew better than to say. I waited for him to give me some kind of look or word that he remember the night a few days past but he showed nothing. I knew better than to hope that he had forgotten.

"Nick? Is that you?" Momma Rose called out in the sweetest voice I ever heard from her.

"Yes, ma'am."

When Momma Rose appeared she had a glow about her. Seeing us watching her, she moved her hands down her sides as if to straighten out some unseen wrinkle. She was nervous. I could see it and it unnerved me a bit. Well that and knowing her date could get me clobbered.

"Are those for me?" she asked, seeing the flowers.

"All but these three," Nick said, removing the three but leaving the rest intact. Momma giggled, actually giggled.

He handed each of us a flower before giving the others to Momma Rose. She smelled them as did Daisy and Thelma. I just looked at Nick. Was he for real? I didn't know what to think but I missed my daddy in that moment more than ever.

"Something wrong May?" he asked.

I shook my head. "I'm fine."

"You sure? You don't like your flower?" I noted that his smile didn't reach his eyes.

"I like it," I said.

"You'll learn that May here is my little rebel. She likes to react differently than most folks."

Her little rebel? What did I rebel against? In my mind Thelma rebelled more than I ever thought to.

"I can see that," Nick joked. Our eyes met again. I got the impression that he wanted to figure me out. Like I was some math calculation that needed answering. Or worse, like an insect he wanted to dissect. A shiver ran down my spine.

"You cold, baby?" Momma Rose asked.

I again shook my head. She then kissed me and Daisy goodbye. Then before they left she told Thelma that the regular rules applied. No parties and no boys. And then they were gone.

* * *

I followed Thelma into the kitchen afterward. Thelma got under the sink and dragged out an old, thick glass vase while I watched her from my perch on the barstool. Thelma was unusually quiet for her.

"So what do you think of Nick?" she asked, filling the vase with water.

"Truth?" I asked.

"Truth," Thelma said, arranging the flowers.

"I don't like him."

Thelma stopped and sighed. Her shoulders sank ever so slightly. "Me neither."

I was thankful that someone agreed with me. Thelma looked up over the flowers. She seemed to be studying me. "What did he do to you?"

"Nothing really," I said. "It's what he could do that scares me. You remember the day Momma Rose lost her night job?"

"Yes."

Torn on how much to confide I shared only what I felt comfortable with. "After you snuck out of the window I went for a walk."

Thelma's eyes widened in disbelief. "May Louise Richards you didn't! Do you know what could have happened to you?"

"Yes, Momma Thelma, I know, but they didn't."

"Who were you with?"

"No one," I said a little too quickly.

"I know better," she said.

She did know better.

"I met a friend."

"A friend? Daisy and I are the only friends you've got around here."

"That's not true. I met a boy at the pool."

She looked as if she was going to argue but changed her tactic instead. "What's his name?"

"Jack," I said defiantly. "Ask Daisy if you don't believe me."

"What were you doing out with this Jack? If Aunt Rose were to find out…"

"I know. That's the problem. Nick saw me walking with my friend."

I said friend so I did not feel as if I was lying to Thelma. Elvis was a boy after all. If Thelma thought it was Jack then so be it. There was a good chance I might never see him again. If I did not, then Thelma may never get to know Jack. But she did know Elvis. If she thought anything was going on she could even tell Momma Rose herself. That would not do.

"That could be a very big problem. What did he say?"

"That's just it. He didn't say anything."

"Maybe he didn't see you," Thelma offered.

"Trust me, he did."

"And he didn't say anything at all?"

I shook my head.

Thelma moved the flowers over to the kitchen table. "If he saw you and hasn't said anything else about it, I would leave it alone. It's clear since you are not dead that he hasn't shared it with Aunt Rose. Maybe he will be cool about it and not say anything."

That was a big difference between the two of us. Thelma pushed bad situations and thoughts from her mind. She said that she would deal with it later and hopefully never. You probably know me by now. I hate open-ended things. I prefer to know the outcome of things as soon as possible. Now I would have to live with Nick having the power to spring this on me (and Momma Rose) at any moment.

# CHAPTER NINE

Momma got home after midnight. I know because I waited up for her. For the longest time Thelma and Daisy stayed awake with me. We played games trying to pass the time. At ten, with eyes drooping and protests of not being tired, Thelma put Daisy to bed. After she got back I was surprised that Thelma did not go out herself. Instead, she spent the next hour or so whispering to Eddie on the telephone.

I camped out on the sofa. After the television stations had signed off for the night I picked up my latest book. One that I borrowed from Thelma that told the story of a peasant girl who falls in love with a prince. Not great literature but I enjoyed it. But as the night wore on I put that aside and turned out the lights. Sleep was about to claim me when I heard voices outside.

I reached over and turned out the light. Snuggling down into the sofa cushions, I pulled the afghan up under my chin and listened. Try as I might, I only received mumblings through the thick oak door for my effort.

The door creaked open, and I heard Momma Rose. "Goodnight."

"Night, Rose," Nick added, sounding sweet, "I'll see you tomorrow?"

"I think that can be arranged."

Tomorrow? What in the world was that about? The date must have went well. There was quiet as Momma Rose closed the door. I heard her keys and purse hitting the table. I laid there. I didn't want her to think that I was spying when in fact that was exactly what I was doing.

Momma Rose came around the sofa and sat down on the coffee table beside me. I held my breath as she pushed a strand of hair from my face. I concentrated on keeping my eyes closed but not clenched. I felt my left one slightly twitch.

"It's no use, May Louise. I know you are awake."

I gave up the ruse. Opening my eyes, I stared up at her.

"You want to tell me what you are doing?"

The truth was out of the question so I spilled the other reason for staying up. "I wanted to know how it went."

"It went well," Momma Rose said.

"Do you like him?"

She took a deep breath and slowly exhaled. "I do."

"Are you going to marry him?"

Momma Rose laughed and held her hands up. "May, I barely know him. I like him, but I'm not sure if I'll ever marry again."

"Why not?"

"I loved your daddy more than the law should allow and he loved me. But our marriage failed miserably. The only things to come from it was you and your sister."

"But aren't you afraid of being alone?"

She glanced down at the hands twisting in her lap. I looked at them too.

"May, you've never had your heart broken before. You've never stood before a preacher and swore forever. Then watched it bit by bit crumble to the ground. That kind of hurting leaves a bitter taste in your mouth."

She had me there. I didn't know those things yet and hopefully never would.

"After that…loneliness pales by comparison. Besides, I've got you and your sister right now. That keep me too busy to think about being alone."

"Do you still love Daddy?"

That question was purely selfish on my part. I wanted to know the answer. I needed to know even though I feared the response. Momma Rose got that pained look a person gets when they want to avoid talking to you about a situation. She bit her lip until I thought it might bleed. She thought a long time before she finally spoke.

"A part of me will always love him. He was my first love and he gave me you and your sister. Even when I get mad I remember that. A part of me will always love him."

I liked it when Momma talked like this. She rarely expressed tender sentiments. Usually it was about the bad things Daisy and I had done or what we should have done. If she was going to be like this after a date with Nick, maybe I would have to rethink having him around.

"So when are you going on another date?"

Momma Rose smiled. "He suggested that we go to the drive-in tomorrow night. His treat."

I sat up. Any bit of sleepiness evaporated from my body. The drive-in for a kid was the bee's knees. You got to be outside (so it's a bit like camping), some have a playground with swings, and you get to see a movie. They also had concession stands that sold food and drink. We never used the concession stand the few times we went in the past. Those times Momma brought our food from home.

"Are you serious?"

She nodded. "All of us. But do not wake your sister. If you tell her now I will never get her back in bed. Do you hear me, May?"

I did and I hated it. How would I go into the bedroom and keep such news to myself? I agreed not to say anything more out of fear of Momma changing her mind if I woke Daisy than anything else.

"Good girl, now it's time for bed."

I followed her down the hall. She reached her doorway ahead of me. She pause to slip off her shoes.

"Night, Momma," I said.

"Good night, sweetheart," she said before going into her room and closing the door.

I was careful not to wake Daisy as I climbed into bed. The window gave off enough light that I could look up and see the ceiling. I thought about my talk with my mother. I would classify it as different from any other conversation we ever had with each other. There was no worry in her brow. No tiredness in her eyes. No vagueness in her countenance. Momma Rose was present in our talk tonight. It had to be because of Nick. He was the only alteration to Momma Rose's normal routine. Maybe I was wrong about him.

Nick had kept my secret from Momma Rose. Maybe he would be a good addition to our family.

* * *

The thermometer hit the century mark the next day. The heat was not the real problem though. Around these parts the dreaded word is humidity. You haven't done anything if you haven't been to Louisville in July. It's muggy before the sun comes up most days. That morning was no different. I estimated it to me in the low eighties for my morning meeting with J.D. I was sweating just sitting there in the swing. My lemonade did nothing to take the edge off.

The heat did not seem to bother J.D. He came out in his dress shirt and slacks like always. The only thing different being he wore a hat today. A navy one that matched his slacks. How did he look so dapper and not die from a heat stroke? I wanted to ask him but didn't because of our unspoken no talk rule.

I also wanted to ask him about Elvis. I had not seen him in the last couple of days and was beginning to get worried. Thelma told me that she saw him when she had snuck out to meet Eddie one night. She said he was walking ahead of her and disappeared down the street before Thelma could catch up to him.

When the house finally awoke Momma Rose put us to cleaning. I mean really worked us. We cleaned cabinets, lined shelves, hung laundry. You name it, we probably did it. I think it was because she knew she had the upper hand with us going to the drive-in that night. I think we were even a little more enthusiastic because none of us wanted to be excluded from the night's festivities.

We finally finished about four that afternoon. That gave time for a late lunch and a nap. After those were completed we prepared for our big night. And it was a big night for our family. Momma Rose turned on the radio and sang each song slightly off key. Daisy and I danced in the middle of the kitchen floor, turning Momma's singing to bouts of laughter. Even Thelma, who thought herself too worldly and grown up, joined in on the fun.

As the sun began to go down I noticed that Momma Rose did grow anxious. Her cheerfulness remained but I knew she wanted the night to go well. She popped a big bucket of popcorn and stuffed it into several bags. After much debating (re: fighting) about who would use Momma's old cowgirl sleeping bag, she settled it by telling us to get a pillow and blanket from our own bed. Then we could lay the sleeping bag on the ground and share it. That satisfied us both.

I had only been to the drive-in a few other times in my life. Once, Daddy took Momma Rose and me the summer before Daisy was born. I remember Momma Rose's belly being big. I got to sit up front and Daddy put his arm around me. I don't remember much more than that. Momma says I asked every question imaginable and Daddy patiently answered every one. She said most of them did not even have to do with the movie. Then about halfway through the movie, I leaned my head against his side and fell asleep.

Daddy drove all the way home with me propped up like that. Momma Rose said it scared her half to death. He drove with one hand on the steering wheel and was more concerned about me waking up than keeping the car on the road. According to Momma, he carried me into the house and tucked me into bed. Now I know it's Momma Rose's memory, but I like to think of it as my own.

    This time the drive-in would be different. Momma Rose said that I could take Daisy to the playground all by myself. She also said that she would give us a dollar to split at the concession stand before the movie started. This night would be different indeed.

# CHAPTER TEN

We must have been quite the sight as we walked out to Nick's car that evening. All of our arms were so full it looked as if we were moving. Thankfully, Nick pulled his sky blue Buick into our driveway. He got out of the car as we approached.

"You girls ready? Think you forgot anything? The kitchen sink maybe?" he teased.

"Ha ha, very funny," Momma Rose said as walked past him. Nick hurried to open the door for her. "Get in, girls."

I started to get in the backseat behind the driver's seat when Thelma stopped me.

"You get in behind Aunt Rose."

Did it really matter what side we sat on? We were going to the same destination and the view would not be any different. The look on my face must have said she was crazy but Thelma did not notice. She climbed into the car and slammed the door. I went to the other side and was forced to wait for Daisy to climb in and get situated.

Nick got in the driver seat and made eye contact with me through the rearview mirror. "Now we are not going to cause any problems tonight. Are we girls?"

Thelma and I both said no while Daisy shook her head.

"Good," he said, firing up the engine, "I can't have my girls acting like a bunch of wild women."

I wanted to ask, when did we become his girls? We were Momma's girls. I even like to think that Daisy and I were Daddy's girls. But Nick's? I looked at the back of Momma Rose's head. I thought that she might correct him, but she did not. Maybe she didn't hear him. Either that or she did not mind Nick using the term. I held out hope that she was going deaf.

***

We were one of the first cars to arrive at the drive-in. The movie screen was hidden off a back road behind some of the biggest oak trees I ever saw. Nick said it was because the owner wanted to keep people who had not paid from seeing the movie. He said that the owner added the fence a year prior after some kids snuck onto the property. I immediately thought of Jack DeWitt.

After making our path around the winding road, we came upon the small ticket office. Nick paid for all of us but not without haggling the guy about paying for Daisy. He told the man that Daisy would be asleep before the first movie was over and that he should only be charged half price for her. The man refused and Nick ended up paying full price for Daisy as well.

As we rounded the corner and the big screen came into view I felt almost giddy. The screen was the largest I had ever seen and I imagined it was one of the biggest in the world. Daisy and I were disappointed when Nick parked the car in the middle of the lot.

"We want to be able to see the whole screen," Nick said when Daisy asked to move closer. Daisy frowned but said nothing.

After a few frantic moments of unloading the car everyone seemed to settle down. Daisy sat coloring a blank piece of paper while Thelma and I lounged on the sleeping bag. Momma Rose sat in a lawn chair talking to Nick who was up on the hood of the car.

To any passersby we would look like any normal family. You know, one of those families you see on television. The kind where a cute kid gets into all sort of any trouble that is wrapped up a half hour. Mom and dad fix everything and all are hugging at the end of the show. I always wanted a family like that but refused to believe that it was possible. Wishing for things only led to heartbreak.

As time went on more and more cars were lining their way into the lot. Others must have believed as Nick. Even though there were dozens of open spot in front of us, we were quickly surrounded on all sides.

"See Daisy," Nick said at the last available spot was filled. Not that Daisy had a clue as to what he was talking about. I decided right then that Nick must not know a whole lot about kids and probably even less about six–year-old girls.

I watched as people got out of their vehicles. Most were young families and couples. One young couple got out of the rusted old pickup truck beside us and held hands as they made their way to the refreshment stand.

"I hope they realize there are children here," Momma Rose said, eyeing the couple.

"If they get out of line I'll be happy to tell them," Nick said, hopping down from the hood. He leaned over Momma Rose and rested his hands on the arms of her chair. "I'll gladly tell them off for you, Momma."

And that was when I saw it. Nick kissed Momma Rose right on the lips. I looked to Daisy and Thelma to see if they noticed but neither were paying attention.

I scooted over to Thelma. "You missed it."

"Missed what?"

I jerked my head toward Momma Rose and Nick.

"What?" Thelma asked, a bit annoyed.

"Nick kissed Momma," I whispered.

Thelma's lip tightened as she looked over her shoulder. Then she looked back to me. "That's what folks do when they are dating. You should know that."

"I do, but it's Momma."

"Aunt Rose is just like the rest of us. Don't you ever dream of kissing a boy?"

"No," but my blush betrayed me.

"You have, haven't you?" Thelma exclaimed, "Who?"

"Nobody."

Thelma grabbed my am and pulled me to her. "May Louise Richards you are lying to me."

I tried to pull back but Thelma would not allow me to. "I am not."

"Your face is so red right now."

"Why is your face red May?" Daisy asked. "You sick?"

"Sick?" Momma Rose said, leaning forward, "Who's sick?"

"May," Daisy said.

"No I'm not," I said, looking up at Momma Rose, "I'm fine. I swear."

"Don't swear. You know I don't like that."

I found that funny considering she swore all the time. I decided not to press my luck and mention it. "I'm fine."

"Come here," she ordered, not believing me. I walked over to her and she held the back of her hand to my forehead. Not satisfied with that she then felt my hands. Momma Rose claimed that she knew we were running a fever by feeling our hands.

"You're not hot but…"

"Momma, I'm fine," I said, hoping the third fine would convince her.

She did not believe me. I could see it in her eyes.

"She's okay," Nick broke the silence, "Probably just excited to be here. Ain't that right May?"

With that last line Nick put a hand on my shoulder. I fought the urge to shrug it off. There was an ickiness that ran down my skin. "That's it. I'm excited."

Momma Rose looked as if she was going to fight us on it and thought better of it. "Okay, but if you're like this in the morning I'm calling Dr. Miller."

"That's fair. Can I go to the concession stand now?" I said. I wanted to get away from her before she rushed us home and ruined all the fun.

"If Thelma goes with you."

I half expected for Thelma to balk. She detested being seen out in public with little kids like me and Daisy. This time, though, was different. She stood up and dusted the dirt and gravel off her shorts. "Whenever you're ready."

I started to walk off when Nick stopped me. "Let me give you girls some money."

"That's okay," I said, "Momma gave me a dollar earlier."

Nick fished around in his front pocket and pulled out a money clip. Counting out five crisp one dollar bills he held his hand out. "Here."

Not sure what to do I looked to Momma Rose for guidance.

"Nick," she said, "You don't have to do that."

"I don't have to do anything. I want to."

"I'll pay you back when I get paid."

"It's my treat. I want the girls to have a good time. And I want them to like me," he added, giving me a wink. Momma smiled and nodded the okay to me. I stood there until Thelma nudged my shoulder.

"Take the money," she said.

So I did. I took the money. I felt strange about taking it but there was nothing else I could do. Thelma and I got several cars away before either of us spoke.

"So what is the guy's name? The one you think of kissing?"

Now, I could continue denying it but Thelma smelled blood. She would not let it go until I told her. She would spend the night badgering me with questions and waiting for me to slip up. My fun night at the movies would be ruined so I decided to give a little.

"You don't know him."

"Then tell me his name. If I don't know him then what would it hurt?"

I took a deep breath and sighed. "Jack, alright? His name is Jack."

"Jack?"

"I told you that you didn't know him," I took a little enjoyment that she seemed disappointed by my admission.

"I just thought it might be someone else."

"Like who?"

Thelma gave me a sideways look. "Like our new neighbor for instance."

Immediately I knew she was speaking of Elvis. "You mean Elvis?"

"Of course Elvis, silly. Who else would I be talking about? He's handsome and a bit dangerous."

Handsome? Yes. Dangerous? That made me grin. He did not seem dangerous to me. Different than most boys his age maybe. A little shy even, but I tried to remember that I had spent more time with him than Thelma. Maybe she misread that quietness as being something more sinister.

"I like Elvis but I wasn't thinking of him."

"Good. He's too old for you and I would hate for you to get your heart broken. And if by some chance he was interest I would have to set him straight. I can't have anyone messing with my kid sister."

Never had Thelma done that before. Never referred to me as anything other than her cousin. Sure, we felt like siblings because we shared a house and were so close in age but not once had we put words like sibling or sister to it. It felt nice. Like I had someone to look out for me the way I tried to look after Daisy. It felt nice.

# CHAPTER ELEVEN

Thelma made our way around the drive-in several times in the next hour. When the speakers came on and the sound of a radio commercial began playing we both jumped. A cheer rumbled through the crowd as the projector came on. I laughed out loud when I saw the dancing hot dogs. Daisy would be loving it. I was about to suggest going back to the car when Thelma spoke again.

"So where did you meet this Jack?"

"I met him at the pool that day." I hoped that she left it at that. To be honest I was afraid of what she would think to hear that he was breaking the rules. Normally Thelma did not care about things like that, but she might this time since she knew I liked him.

"Do you think that you will see him again?"

I shook my head. "What are the odds of that happening? Kids that go to that pool probably go to seven different schools."

"You never know. Look at Eddie and me. Six months and two moves and we're still going strong."

"Where is Eddie? I thought he would meet you here."

"I told him not to come."

"Why?" That was not like Thelma.

"I don't know. I just did." She shrugged.

Now I was the dog with the bone. Or twenty questions. "Are you made at him?"

"Why would I be mad at him?" Thelma said, deflecting my question with one of her own.

"I don't know. That's just what people ask. Are you sure he didn't do anything?"

"No, he didn't do anything," Thelma said, looking around to make certain no one paid us any attention. "I told him to stay away so I could keep an eye on things tonight."

"Oh," I said, wanting her to think that I understood what she meant. I did not by the way.

"I wanted to keep an eye on Nick. You know, make sure everything went well."

"Are you afraid Daisy and I are going to muck things up?"

"Not exactly. I—" Thelma started to say only to be cut off by a black-headed greaser.

"Hey beautiful," the greaser said, getting out of the driver side of an old jalopy. "You looking for a good time?"

"Dream on asshole," Thelma said. "Come on May."

"What did you call me?" the teenager said, getting closer. He was what Momma Rose called a meathead. Heavy-set with no neck and reeked of, I inhaled again, weed and pepperoni. Don't ask me how I know about weed just know that I do.

*Weed and pepperoni, what a weird combination*, I thought.

Thelma stopped in front of his car and placed her hands on her hips. Like Momma, Thelma rarely backed down from a fight. "Are you deaf as well? I called you an asshole."

I stood between the two like a deer in the headlights. A small crowd of teenagers gathered around us. Neither one could back down now and save face. The greaser looked at me.

"You're lucky you've got your kid sister with you."

"Why?" Thelma rolled her eyes. "She could kick your ass, too, if she wanted."

I did not know who Thelma was talking about but it positively was not me. I wanted to hit her with a baseball bat for even suggesting such a thing. The greaser was easily twice my size. I could tell from the snickering in the crowd more than a few others found the idea hilarious. The greaser looked around. We all knew that he was losing the mob.

"You're those new kids over on Haywood aren't you?"

"What's it to you?"

The greaser raised his chin and pushed out his lower lip. I think he was trying to look tough but he reminded me of a pouting baby. "Nothing. Just that I hear your mother ain't nothing but a whore of a divorcee. You sure you aren't just like her?"

"You take that back," I shouted at him.

"What are you going to do about?" he laughed and turned his back on me.

Now I will never be able to explain my next moves. They went by in a blur. I doubt there was any logical reasoning and given any thought I would most likely never do it again.

I attacked him.

My first punch was a closed fist to the dead center of the greaser's back. I think I hurt my hand more than I did him. But I did catch him by surprise and he took a step forward. As he turned around and I realized the danger I was in from the angry look on that ugly face I almost ran. Almost. He did insult my mother. I had heard similar comments before, of course. Not directly mind you. I find that most people would rather gossip behind your back. But like I said, I had heard those whisperings before and this boy was no different. He just was on the receiving end of my anger.

"Take it back," I said again.

"Or what?"

Instead of giving him an answer. I lunged at him. Without the element of surprise he easily deflected most of my punches. The ones that did connect had little, if any, effect. I kept throwing them anyway. The circle of people pushed closer and I think Thelma joined in. Either that or she was trying to pull me away. It was a toss up as to which since I was lost in the melee.

The greaser grabbed me so hard by the hair that I saw stars. He swung me around as my arms flapped out to my sides. Out of my peripheral vision I saw him push Thelma. Whatever he planned next was forever halted by another body being forced between us. The surprised greaser let go and I fell to the ground. I immediately began rubbing my head and checking to see that he had not pulled me bald headed. As I felt around on my scalp I was thankful that most of it was still there.

"Didn't your momma teach you any better?" Elvis said. He had been the one to come to our rescue. He pushed the greaser up against the car and his forearm was across the boy's neck. The greaser could not speak with Elvis crushing his windpipe and he held several more seconds before letting go. The meathead doubled over and started gasping for air.

"Who the hell are you?" he asked between gulps.

"I'm the guy you are going to have to deal with if you mess with these girls again. You got that?"

"Yeah man. I hear you. Besides, she started it," he said, pointing to me.

Elvis looked down and gave me a grin and a wink. Then turned back to the greaser.

"Then I suggest you leave her alone."

With the fight concluded, the mob went back to other things. The greaser walked over to talk to a few of his friends. He wasn't happy but he wasn't doing anything about it either. Elvis held out a hand that I gratefully took ahold of and pulled myself up.

"You all right, May?" Thelma asked, checking to make sure that I was unharmed.

I nodded so she turned to Elvis. "Thank you."

"It was nothing," Elvis tilted his head down and appeared uncomfortable.

"It was," Thelma said softly before asking me, "Isn't it?"

"No one's ever taken up for us like that," I said.

"Then it was my pleasure. But tell me one thing, pet?"

"What?"

"What was that fight about?"

"He insulted Momma Rose."

"Not to mention me and you," Thelma chimed in.

Meeting Elvis's gaze I saw the understanding in his eyes. Without a word he knew that it was not about me or Thelma. I could handle or better yet ignore a jab at me or Thelma. I could not let the greaser slur Momma Rose's good name and Elvis knew that. I also knew that he approved.

"I would have done the same thing if he had been talking about my momma."

"But that's different," Thelma said. "You're a boy."

Elvis placed his hands in his pockets. "Why is that different? Besides the obvious?"

"She could have gotten hurt."

"Pet, are you hurt?"

"No," I said. Which was mostly the truth. My head hurt where the meathead had pulled my hair and my bottom hurt from the fall. Otherwise I was fine.

"What if you had? What would you have told Aunt Rose? Would it have been worth it if you were sitting in a hospital at the end of the night?"

There was no answer for that nightmare. Once I recovered Momma Rose would have gladly slaughtered me. Or grounded me until I was thirty. Or both.

"Sure she took more risk being a girl but she should have done it none the less," Elvis said.

I saw another argument brewing between these two so I decided to get between them. The fact that they seemed to be getting to know each other did not sit well with me either. I guess since I thought of Elvis as my own the green-eyed monster was rearing its ugly head.

"Thelma, stop. Remember that he was helping us."

"It's fine, pet. But if you two are all right I'm going to be shoving off."

"Do you have to?" I whined.

"You keep out of trouble, you hear me?"

He smiled that smile that didn't quite reach his eyes but melted my heart regardless. He then looked up into the night sky. "You know, you should go stargazing tomorrow night. I have a feeling there may be a shooting star."

I got his message loud and clear. He wanted to meet again. I thought of Momma Rose and how I would have to sneak out again. "I don't know. Tomorrow night might be too cloudy."

"I guess we will have to wait and see. A pleasure to see you again Thelma."

Thelma blushed and stuttered slightly when she spoke. "Good night Elvis and thanks again."

And with that he walked off.

"What an odd bird," Thelma stated more to the world at large than me in particular.

"He's not odd. He's just Elvis."

Thelma fanned herself with her hand. Clearly it was more than the heat that was getting to her. A doctor would have diagnosed her with a case of Elvis. And why not? He defended us when no one else had. Like a hero I read about so often in my books. Only Elvis lived outside the pages of a novel. He was a real, live, breathing hero and like all heroes he rescued the damsel in distress, me.

I liked stories like that.

# CHAPTER TWELVE

Word of my tumble with the greaser got out fast. I got congratulations from a few of Thelma's friends that she introduced me to. It was weird how I felt both extremely young and grown up at the same time. I was the youngest kid by far but none of Thelma's friends treated me that way. Most of them were in high school but they acted as if I was one of them. I was reminded of the woman who went and lived among the monkeys in Africa (or someplace equally far away). The chimps treated the lady as one of their own. Tonight I was that lady.

I didn't ask Thelma why. Momma Rose said that would be looking a gift horse in the mouth and I was not about to do that. The only thing that stopped Thelma was that she refused to let me try a cigarette. Now mind you I have taken a few puffs of Momma Rose's when she was not looking. Not that Momma Rose smoked a lot. She only lit one up on Saturdays when she cleaned the house and usually only took a puff or two. Mostly the cigarette would burn. Thelma did not know I had done that, and when one of her female friends took a drag and passed it to me she grabbed it out of my hands.

"Are you crazy May?" she said, stomping it into the ground. "We come back and Aunt Rose smells tobacco on your breath she would skin us both."

"Relax," the friend said, "it's not like she was going to inhale or nothing."

"She's eleven Sandy."

Sandy cringed. "Sorry, I didn't know."

"Well now you do."

I folded my arms across my chest. Did Thelma really have to remind everyone of my age? It hardly seemed fair. I didn't keep telling them that she was only sixteen. Instead I pivoted around and looked up at the movie screen. The film was Titanic. I knew that only because we saw the title on the way in. On the screen was two men in uniform talking to one another. Judging from the concerned looks on their faces they must have hit the iceberg already.

"I bet they paid more than a dime to get on that boat."

I looked to my left. It was Jack. He was walking toward me. I started to smile but remembered how he left me the other day. I shut my mouth tight and looked back at the screen. I didn't really see what was going on but I did not want him to think that I was interested. Elvis said to play hard to get and that was exactly what I intended to do.

"That's the way you're going to be?" He stopped right next to me. "And here I thought we were friends."

I turned my head toward him. I looked him up and down with a serious look. Not impressed, he actually laughed at me. "I'm sorry, alright?"

I rolled my eyes. He continued. "I shouldn't have said what I did."

"Okay," I said, rather happy with the iciness in my tone. I patterned it on the times that Eddie fell out of favor with Thelma. "But you shouldn't have said what you did either."

That got me going. "And why not? I was just being honest."

"That's just it. Girls don't talk like that."

Another male telling me how a girl should behave. Maybe there was something to it. I decided to go a different route. "It doesn't matter now. I don't like you."

"Sure you do," Jack said.

"No I do not."

"You don't?"

"Something you should know about girls…we change our minds and we change them often."

That seemed to confuse him. Seriously? This playing hard to get worked? "You weren't interested so I moved on."

"Well…good," only it didn't sound as if he was sure about that.

"What are you doing here tonight?"

"Brain surgery," he teased, "I came to see a movie."

"Oh," I said. We stood there for a moment. Neither saying anything. I searched my head to come up with anything clever to keep the conversation going. "Did you come here alone?"

"No," Jack pointed back to his left, "my brothers are around here somewhere."

"And did you cut a hole in the fence this time?"

"No, we've got a spring and fall ticket."

"I thought that the drive-ins were summers only?"

Thelma took notice of us and decided to join the conversation at that point. "May, he doesn't have a ticket. They spring up onto the fence and fall to the other side. Jack Dewitt what in the hell are you doing out here tonight?"

Jack inspected the ground as if he had lost something.

"Wait a minute," I said, "Do you two know each other?" Thankfully I knew that Thelma would never got out with a younger boy. It would crush me to think that maybe the two had a "thing" at some point.

"Jack is Eddie's little brother."

You could have knocked me over with a feather. When people say it's a small world you never really believe it until it is proven with a situation like this. "I didn't even know Eddie had a brother."

"We're half-brothers," Jack said as if that would explain it all. It did explain the physical differences. While Jack was blond and lean, Eddie could be describe as nothing other than big and dark.

"Really?"

Jack nodded. "We have the same dad."

"I thought Eddie told you about sneaking into places without paying," Thelma said, sounding like she does with me and Daisy, "And where is Rascal?"

Rascal? That surely could not be a given name.

"He's around here somewhere. He told me that he was going to meet up with his girl."

"I swear you boys are going to be the death of me and Eddie. Just stay out of trouble tonight, you hear me?"

"Yes, ma'am." Jack gave her a mock salute and I busted into giggles. Thelma gave us both a dirty look and then stopped. I do not know what she saw but I know that she did not like it. "What's going on here?"

"Nothing," Jack and I answered in unison.

"Jack..." Thelma said in a way that let me know that she was thinking about our earlier conversation.

"Yeah?" he answered.

"Nothing. May walk to the ladies room with me."

"I don't have to go."

"But I do."

That, as they saw, was the end of that. I looked helplessly at Jack.

"I'll just wait here for you."

I smiled and nodded before joining Thelma for the jaunt to the ladies room. With the movie playing there were only a few women. Thelma walked over to the mirror and began primping her hair.

"Jack has a lot of problems, May. Problems that are too much for a little kid like you."

I followed her to the mirror. My hair was pulled back in a ponytail so there was not much primping I could do. I stared at my reflection in the mirror. "I'm not a little kid."

Thelma stopped and looked at me in the mirror. "Trust me on this one."

"It's not like I'm going to marry him," I countered.

"You never know."

In my imagination I saw me in a white wedding gown with matching gloves walking to the aisle of a church I'd seen in a movie once. My future husband would be there in a black tux, his hair neatly brushed back with the perfect amount of gel. My wedding ring would be a gold band with a matching diamond engagement ring. Momma Rose sat in the front row quietly crying into a handkerchief. It was all elegant and pretty in my head. I had that dream for years but for the first time my future husband was not imaginary. He looked exactly like Jack. It was Jack's beaming baby blues and dimples I saw staring back at me.

"Earth to May," Thelma said, waving a hand in front of my face.

"What did you say?"

Thelma sighed and went back to the mirror. "Eddie doesn't like his dad much."

I did not think much of that. There were millions of people who do not like their parents and most of them were teenagers. "You don't get along with your parents."

"You're right. I don't get along with them but I do like them. I love them."

Thelma surprised me. Thelma rarely talked about her parents. We never saw them and she never talked to them. There were no visits either way. Momma Rose was more of a parent to Thelma in my opinion. But the only opinion that mattered was Thelma's.

"Are you saying that Jack hates his dad?"

"No, I'm saying that Eddie hates him. Jack loves him and tries his hardest to protect him."

"What's the problem with that?"

Thelma shrugged her shoulders. "It's not if the parent is worth a crap. Eddie's dad isn't. He drinks too much and from what Eddie says he's not a fun drunk."

I thought about that for a minute. If what Thelma told me was true how sad was it for Jack? I almost wished that she hadn't of told me. Now I would have to go back out there and pretend to Jack that I did not know something I most definitely did. She put that on my shoulders and probably did not even realize it. Thelma thought that she was helping the situation.

"I doubt I'll even meet his daddy. We're not like you and Eddie. I'm only twelve."

"You're eleven."

I slapped Thelma on the arm. "I'm almost twelve. You might as well say twelve."

Thelma smiled. "Oh, you've told Jack that you're twelve, haven't you?"

"I might have," I said. "So you won't tell him will you?"

I held my breath.

"I won't go out of my way to tell him but if he asks, May, I won't lie. You understand me?"

I nodded. "I do. Thank you, Thelma."

"Just be careful, you hear me?"

I did. I heard her even though I didn't think there was anything to be careful about.

***

After talking a few minutes more, we headed back outside. Jack was standing with a group of boys about his age. I thought that he had forgotten his promise to wait for me. Thelma was at my side. "If you are going to do this train wreck, then do it right. Make him notice you."

"I'm eleven, I don't know how to make him notice me," I said.

"May, haven't I taught you anything? You need to be self-confident. Show him that he would be lucky to be with a girl like you."

67

"That's easy for you to say, you've got those," I pointed at Thelma's double D's. I tilted my head down at my own chest, "Mine have barely began to grow."

"Darlin', it doesn't matter as long as you have them. Boys love them. Besides you don't need these. You have this face," she touched my cheek, "and a good heart."

Now I knew that boys didn't fall in love with a good heart at first sight. A pretty face, maybe, but never a girl's personality. That doesn't even happen in fairytales. Even in *Beauty and the Beast* you can guess who the looker is and it is not the Beast. It was nice to hear though and a bit of a confidence booster.

"And don't look now but you have caught someone's attention."

She was right. Jack had stopped talking with his friends and was looking directly at me. I mean us. I mean…me?

I smiled at him and quickly looked away. If was as if looking at him was too much for me.

"Jack's got a girlfriend," one of his friends said, making kissing noises. Jack pushed the boy and he staggered back, laughing. A few of the other joined in but Jack didn't pay them any attention as he walked up to me.

"Don't listen to those guys."

"I'm not."

"So you want to go and get some popcorn or something?"

"Sure," I said. "If that's okay with Thelma."

Thelma nodded and spoke to Jack. "There and back, you hear me?"

"Yeah, yeah."

"I'll wait for you. Do not make me come looking for you May."

"I won't."

Jack walked beside me to the concession stand. There was a good two feet between us but I felt as if we were almost touching. I stole a glance at him and my heart skipped. I looked down at my shoes to think. I don't know why I thought it would make things different. With him out of my sight my other senses came to life. Breathe, I told myself. Calm down, he is just a boy.

*A boy you like,* I thought. *Definitely a boy I liked.*

Neither of us had said a word as we reached the concession building. Jack held the door open for me and I managed to eke out a "Thank You."

That seemed to ease things somewhat. We walked over to the counter. A little old lady with a hairnet and a cigarette hanging out of her mouth was working the counter.

"What do you want?" she barked between drags.

"A small popcorn," Jack said, leaning a hip against the counter and held up two fingers, "and two sodas."

The woman shook her head and turned her back to us.

"So I hear that you're a fighter."

"Excuse me?"

"A couple of those asshole friends back there said that you took on three greasers tonight."

"Three?" I asked, stunned at how much the story had blown up in such a short amount of time, "It wasn't three and it wasn't much of a fight. He was bothering Thelma."

When Jack frowned he got a worry line on his forehead right between his eyes. I fought the urge to reach up and smooth it out for him. "I should have guessed that part."

"She wasn't doing anything. Honest she wasn't."

"This time. I like Thelma and all, but she brings a lot of trouble on herself."

"I don't disagree, but this time she was minding her own business."

"What were you all doing anyway?" he asked. The old lady brought our food back to the counter. She kept it out of reach until Jack reached into his pocket and pulled out a small wad of rolled up bills. There was a worn rubber band instead of the gold clip that Nick used.

"Just walking," I said. "I'm surprised you didn't pay with a bag full of dimes."

Jack got his change and tossed the few pennies into an empty jar marked "Tips". "I roll the change up and take it to the bank on Fridays. They cash it out for me."

"Well thank you for spending your money on me," I said as Jack handed me a drink and grabbed his own and the popcorn.

"You're welcome. I wouldn't do it for just any girl."

I blushed but hid it behind my cup as I took a big gulp. Unfortunately, the liquid went down the wrong pipe and burned all the way down. I began coughing. You know those big sputtering coughs that make people stare at you like you have the plague. After the initial coughing jag was over I took another sip of the offending soda. I coughed a few more times but not as loud nor as long. To Jack's credit he did not look mortified at the gapes I was getting from the crowd. He looked genuinely worried.

"You okay?" he asked when I was finally done.

I bobbed my head still fearing another coughing fit if I spoke too soon.

He walked over to an empty picnic table and sat down. "Let's rest here awhile."

"But we told Thelma that we would be right back."

"So she'll think there is a line. By my calculations that gives us about five more minutes before we need to head back."

I hesitated and he saw it.

"Come on, May," Jack said. patting the seat beside him, "you know you want to."

I moved closer. "I don't want to get in trouble, though."

Jack rested his elbows on the table and began eating. "Because you sat down with me for five minutes?"

"Yes."

"Okay, but I would be more worried about your mom finding out about that fight."

I sank down on the bench beside him. "You don't think anyone will tell her, do you?"

"No, I just wanted you to sit down," he laughed.

I wanted to be mad at him. I wanted to, but it was impossible. Did I mention he had the cutest dimples that I just wanted to reach out and touch? What was wrong with me? I'm so not a touchy feely person!

"Popcorn?" he held the bag out to me/ but I shook my head, "You sure? It's pretty tasty."

"No thanks. It gets stuck in my teeth."

He popped in a few more kernels. You don't know what you are missing out on."

"I've had popcorn before. I like the taste. I just hate how my teeth feel after I eat it."

"Smile for me."

I did and Jack studied me. His eyes meeting mine when he was done. "You have the most beautiful smile I have ever seen."

"I bet you say that to all the girls."

"You've got me there. I do say it. But you know what, May? I like yours better."

"Is this where I swoon and you promise me your undying love?"

"I could but I won't."

"Because you will be leaving here someday?" I teased, but Jack took me seriously.

"Not someday. Five years. Then the day I turn eighteen I'm out of here."

The belief in his eyes was only out shadowed by the darkness that he seemed desperate to keep from me. Desperate to hide from the world.

"I don't know about five years. We tend to move a lot. But I could help you fill up some of that time if you want."

"I think you are already doing that," he whispered, looking at my lips.

The air went out of my lungs and the world melted away as he looked at me. As inexperienced as I was I knew that he was about to kiss me. My first real kiss (mind if you didn't count the sloppy kiss I shared with Herman at Molly Freeman's birthday party last year when we played spin the bottle in her parent's basement. No Herman's kiss didn't count because he was thin with a stutter and acne. The only reason I kissed him was I didn't want to look like a baby. Well that and it was spin the bottle and I did want to know about kissing. It wasn't much come to think of it and it inspired none of the feelings that I felt at the moment just thinking about Jack's kiss. No, Herman did not count. Jack would be my first kiss.

And Jack would be my first kiss but not that night. Just as we leaned in toward one another, I heard my name at a time and in a way no child ever wanted to be called.

"May Louise Richards just what in the hell are you doing?"

If the ground would have opened up and swallowed me whole I would have been eternally grateful. But nope the universe must work for Momma Rose. Because the earth did not open up and Jack and I were left to deal with Momma.

"Momma," I jumped to my feet almost knocking my drink to the ground. As it was the drink tilted and several huge drops plopped onto the picnic table.

Momma Rose looked as pissed as I had ever seen her. That was pretty mad. Jack however stood up and held out his hand. "Hello Mrs. Richards. I'm Jack Dewitt, it's a pleasure to finally meet you, ma'am. I feel like I already know you after all the good things that May here has said about you."

*What a cool liar,* I thought considering I had said very little about Momma Rose at all. Momma did not seem to be buying it but she shook his hand anyway.

"I wish the same could be said about you, son. We're leaving now. Come on May."

I gave an apologetic look. Jack covered my hand with his under the table. I watched as he took a deep breath and faced Momma Rose. "I would like it very much if I could drop by your house some time Mrs. Richards so that we may become better acquainted."

"You can do that son but I doubt it will get you anywhere with my eleven year old daughter."

Jack immediately let go and I missed the heat. A cruel triumphant grin broke at the corners of Momma Rose's lips. She had guessed my lie. I instantly went into action and began explaining myself. "I'll be twelve next month and you said you just turned thirteen last week."

"Come along May," Momma Rose said, not waiting to see if I followed.

"Jack, please look at me."

He did but I didn't like what I saw there. The accusation was deep. I had lied to him and he hadn't expected it. I covered his hand this time and gave it a squeeze. "I'm sorry."

I hurried after Momma Rose knowing that I may have lost something I just discovered. My heart ached at the notion and would hurt for a long time.

## CHAPTER THIRTEEN

Not one word did Momma Rose utter on the walk back. Then when we arrived at the car it was even worse. Her mood was black and everyone saw it. I took a seat on the sleeping bag beside Daisy. Thankfully she had already went to sleep.

I sat there with my knees to my chest with my chin on my arms. Fear and heartbreak ran rampant through my veins. One fighting the other to win control of my emotions. I did not dare look to see if Mamma Rose was watching. I knew she was. It was as if I could feel her eyes searing into my back.

After a while I gave up and laid down beside Daisy and closed my eyes. Nick had placed one of the speakers on the ground so I concentrated on the voices coming from the film. Depressed, I began to drift off myself when I head Momma Rose say my name. I was about to lift my head up when I realized that she was not getting my attention. She was talking to Nick about me. She thought I was asleep. I hoped that listening would give me some insight into how to handle her.

"So I walk up and she is sitting with a boy. A boy, Nick."

"She's almost a teen, Rose," Nick said. "You ain't going to stop that. Boys come with that."

Maybe my gut misjudged Nick. I never guessed that he would ever defend me to Momma Rose. "Especially with that wild niece of yours serving as mentor."

"Thelma is a good girl."

"She is wild as a buck and you know it. May and Daisy are watching and learning from her."

"I know," Momma Rose said, "but back to May. I think that I came upon them before anything happened. Can you believe that he had the nerve to ask to come to my house and get better acquainted?"

"Well you can be assure that he's not an idiot," Nick said.

"And why is that? Because he thought to try and kiss up to me? I don't think so. She is too young and I intend to tell her about it tomorrow."

"Why not tell her now?"

I almost lifted my head off the ground in my attempt to hear Momma Rose's next words. She paused long enough that I wasn't sure that she was even going to answer. But she did.

"Because I'm not sure what I'm going to tell her yet."
***

My pretend sleep gave way to the real thing and Momma Rose woke me up as Thelma walked up. Thelma had remained missing until the credits began to roll on the final film of the night. Nick bent down and picked up the sleeping Daisy and put her in the backseat.

Thelma tried speaking to Momma Rose only to get shot down with one word answers. She began to say something to me and I quickly shook my head. Thelma got the hint and began helping us clean up. When we finished we all got back in the car and Nick drove us home.

It was the longest car ride that I can ever remember in my life.

By the time we got home it as after two a.m. Daisy woke up as Nick pulled the car into the driveway. Thelma and I quickly herded her into the house with our belongings before she started asking questions. Momma Rose stayed outside with Nick. I don't know what they did but I bet it was the same thing she got upset at me and Jack for almost doing.

"What happened to you? I told you to go to the concession building and come right back," Thelma whispered as I climbed into bed.

"We did. We had stopped for a minute and the next thing I know Momma Rose is standing there."

"What were you doing?"

"Nothing," I mumbled, punching my pillow.

Thelma didn't believe me. She didn't say anything and just waited.

"Okay," I said, "we had just got our popcorn and drinks. You know those picnic tables? We stood there for a minute. Jack was just about to kiss me when Momma Rose walked up."

"Oh lord," Thelma said. "No wonder she is mad. I told you two to go there and come right back. If you would have listened to me she would have missed you entirely."

"I don't need to hear I told you so."

"Well I did. May, you don't know how to be a bad girl. You need to follow the rules."

"I wasn't trying to be a bad girl." Maybe I was a little bit but not enough to get in trouble. I needed help now to figure out what to do to minimize the damage. "Jack asked if he could come by the house and Momma Rose basically told him no."

"She didn't."

I nodded my head against the pillow. "That's not even the worst of it. She told Jack that I was only eleven. After that he wouldn't talk to me."

"He will probably never talk to you again."

"Thanks." That made me feel worse. Even though I've spent the last few hours thinking the exact same thing.

"It's true."

"Just tell me what I need to do."

Thelma sighed. "You need to learn from this. I'm not going to sugarcoat it for you. I know Jack and he doesn't do rules well. He does parents even less. If Aunt Rose was as nasty as you said I doubt he will bother with you again. The fact that you lied and are eleven isn't helping your cause either."

"What about Momma Rose?"

Thelma propped her head up on her arm. "That is going to be way trickier. You're on her radar now. My advice is to do nothing."

"Nothing?"

"Yes. You just pretend that nothing happened."

"Okay, what if Momma Rose says something?"

"You're on your own there. It depends on what she says. My advice is that you stay quiet and let her say her piece. If you try and defend yourself it will just turn out ugly. Trust me, I learned that one the hard way."

I had about a million other questions for Thelma but she rolled over and gave me her back. "Goodnight."

What was so good about? I doubted that there would be good nights ever again.

***

J.D. missed our Sunday morning meeting again. I watched the house next door for any sign of life and movement but there was nothing. This morning I brought my bowl of cereal and had breakfast as the sun came up. I tried reading my book but with the previous night's activities it proved futile. I tried several times before giving up entirely.

I sat listening to the quiet when the back door opened and Momma Rose came out. She held a cup of coffee in her hand. I watched without speaking as she walked over to me and sat down on the swing beside me. My anxiety grew as we sat there, neither of us saying a word. Momma Rose seemed to be gathering her nerve or her thoughts. Me? I was just following Thelma's advice and waiting for her to lower the boom on me.

"May, what happened last night…I wasn't prepared for. I think of you as a little girl. My little girl."

"But Momma—" I started. Thelma's instruction went out the window.

"I know you're not a little girl," Momma turned toward me.

"I know that there will be boys. But you listen and listen to me good. You will not act like Thelma. There won't be a parade of parties and different boys traipsing through your life. Do you understand that?"

I bobbed my head. That was the last thing I sought. I wanted to tell Momma Rose that but was too afraid. I wanted to explain that I wanted love. Real love. The kind of love that grew old together. I wanted tell Momma a lot of things but those things were held hostage by my fear.

"I still don't want you seeing that boy. For one thing, he is too old for you. For another… he looks like trouble." Momma Rose took a drink of her coffee.

"He's not," I said not quite believing myself.

"I've said what I came out here to say. I do not want to have this conversation again."

Thelma was right. Arguing with Momma Rose wouldn't lead me anywhere I wanted to go. So I gave up. "Okay."

Momma Rose sat there a few minutes more. We were inches apart and I never felt more isolated from her than in that moment. The heat that already began to burn the morning could not warm the chill in my heart.

"There will be other boys. Good ones who will love you. Ones that will take care of you."

I had a feeling that she was no longer talking about Jack. If you asked me she was not talking about Daddy either. I think she spoke of Nick. That gave me pause. He seemed cool but there was that nagging sensation that I should not trust him.

"I know," I said, because I knew it was what she wanted to hear. Also because Jack probably hated me and would never speak to me again. Momma Rose put her arm around me and gave me a hug. I knew that I had answered her right.

\*\*\*

You remember Elvis asking me in code to meet him Sunday night? Well that didn't happen. In fact I never left the yard that day. I knew that Momma Rose was watching me. I think that she was looking for cracks. You know, any signs that I was like Thelma and would sneak off the first opportunity I got.

I wanted to show her that I could be trusted. I helped out with the wash and hung it out to dry on the clothes line. I played with Daisy and kept her occupied while Momma took an afternoon nap. I even did the lunch dishes. Meeting with Elvis was just too much of a risk this close to what happened with Jack. I hoped he understood. While I did the above mentioned items I kept an eye out the window for him though. I saw Vera go out and come back with groceries but never saw J.D. or Elvis.

That evening Nick came over for dinner and we ate as a family. All of us, even Thelma. I thought it went okay. Nick did most of the talking. He told us stories about people he knew. It did not matter that we had no clue as to who these people were because each story was hilarious. By the end of dinner my jaws hurt from laughing so much.

For dessert we all had a piece of Momma Rose's pumpkin pie and sat in the living room and ate like grown-up. Well, all of us except Daisy. She made a mess with most food and Momma Rose told her that she didn't want to have to clean pumpkin out of the carpet. So Daisy sat at the table.

After we finished Thelma went off to our room. Momma Rose and Nick sat on the couch watching *I Love Lucy* on the television. Daisy sat between them playing with her dolls. I, meanwhile, reclined in the chair reading.

"You know I could get use to this," Nick said to Momma Rose.

"You could? It's not always like this. The girls are on their best behavior because you are here. Normally they are hanging from the rafters by now."

Nick reached over and ruffled Daisy's hair. She shot him a dirty look that he did not seem to notice. "I don't care. I like it here."

Momma rested her head on the back of the couch. "We like having you here. I just wished that the real world wasn't calling us both tomorrow. I hate to think of going back to work."

"If things go as planned maybe you won't have to do it much longer."

Momma Rose smiled at that. I sat up. Things between Momma Rose and Nick were moving way faster than anticipated. I mean, were they really talking about marriage? After two dates? Maybe I needed to talk to Momma Rose more than she needed to have that talk with me this morning. I decided to break it up.

"Momma Rose is it okay if Daisy and I walk to the library tomorrow?"

"I don't know," Momma Rose said. "What is that? Like twelve blocks?"

I held up where I was in my book to show that I was almost finished. "I need to check out new books and get a couple for Daisy too. We'll be careful."

"I guess, but—" Momma said.

"I can take them," Nick said in a surprising offer.

"You will?" both me and Momma Rose said.

Nick nodded, "Sure. I don't have to be to work until one tomorrow. I could take the girls in the morning and that would still give me enough time. That's if you and the girls don't mind."

"Of course we don't mind. Do we girls?" And with that Nick just solidified his status with Momma Rose. Even if I hated the man I could not say that I didn't want him to take us. It wasn't nice and Momma might get the wrong impression about me going to the library. Unlike Thelma, I would have actually gone to the library. But I wouldn't have minded walking. Especially if on the way I had ran into Jack and was "forced" to speak with him.

"That's fine if you want to take us Nick."

"Good. I will be here at ten a.m. sharp."

With that settled I sat back and started reading again. I was right in the middle of an epic sea battled when I heard Daisy exclaim, "But I don't want to go to bed. I'm not even tired."

Daisy never wanted to go to bed and we had to fight with her every single night. I looked up at the clock on the mantle 8:30 p.m.

That was a little early even for Daisy. Momma Rose was feeling brave.

"Nick's right, you need to rest," Momma Rose said.

"I don't want to," Daisy said, crossing her arms and holding her breath.

"Now Daisy," Nick said, sitting up. He remained utterly calm but I could tell that he was getting put out. "You can hold your breath, scream, and cry, but I'm telling you that when you are done you are going to bed."

Wow, where did that come from? Nick was telling Daisy what to do now?

"May," Nick said to me, "take your sister and put her to bed, please."

He said please but I knew that I didn't really have a choice. I got to my feet. "Come on Daisy."

"No," Daisy said, exhaling the held breath and just as quickly inhaled again.

I leaned over to take her hand. Daisy threw herself back on the couch and lifted her legs up kicking. Why did she have to make this hard? Daisy was easygoing when it came to everything else.

"Daisy please," Momma Rose pleaded.

"You know a good ass busting would cure her of this," Nick told Momma Rose. Daisy's eyebrows went up an inch but she didn't budge otherwise. I implored her to concede with my eyes. There was nothing good that could come from this. It wasn't like Thelma or I would tell if she did not go to sleep once behind the closed bedroom door.

Daisy shook her head at me. Why did she have to take a stand here? To my mind it was not worth it. I thought her insane to rock the boat over this matter. "Come on, Daisy, I'll let you read a few pages out of my book before you go to sleep."

"You never let me read your stuff."

"I will tonight and tomorrow we will find you a book in the big kids section."

"Can I pick it out?"

I knew where she was headed. A few weeks prior Daisy had found one of Thelma's romance novels. She was halfway through the *Duke and the Peasant Girl* before I caught her and took the book away.

Nick looked impatient and Momma Rose did not seem too happy either. Daisy knew that she had me right where she wanted me. What I think she failed to realize was that she was in a very perilous situation. Momma Rose and Nick both looked ready to explode.

"Yes. Yes, now come on."

Satisfied, Daisy got to her knees and kissed Momma Rose on the cheek. "Night, Momma."

She then turned to Nick and did the same thing. "Night, Nick."

And just like that the tension in the room vanished. Nick and Momma Rose smiled at each other. I rolled my eyes as Daisy bounced down the hallway. It was hard to stay mad at the kid.

"I'll be back after I get her asleep," I said.

"Good night May," Momma Rose said as I began to follow after Daisy. I looked over my shoulder like she had lost her mind. "It's only eight-thirty."

"But by the time you get Daisy settled it will be after nine."

"And you need your rest as well," Nick said.

*Whatever,* I thought, *you're not my dad.* I just was not brave enough to voice that opinion. Instead I said nothing and went off to my bedroom. Meeting Elvis that night was not a risk I was willing to take. There would be other nights.

# CHAPTER FOURTEEN

The next morning Daisy, Nick, and I jumped into his car and made our way to the library. Nick did not go in with us. Instead he said that he would wait in the car but that we needed to hurry up. Daisy and I went running across the street and hurried up the flight of steps and inside.

The Oakdale Library was a big building. Daisy headed off in the direction of the children's section while I checked in our books with the librarian. After doing that I walked up and down the new fiction wall. I'm not much into non-fiction books. The fact is that they bore me to no end. I learned about real things in history class. That was enough for me…for now.

After picking up more than a dozen new books, reading the backs and placing them back on the shelf, I decided to go get lost in the stacks. I loved looking at the books. I really loved the smell of paper. I could stay here for days but was aware of the fact that Nick was waiting in the car for us. I made a couple of selections before I saw the biggest, thickest book I had ever seen in my life. That was a book that could keep me busy the rest of the summer. It was blue with black lettering on the spine.

Gone With the Wind. I immediately recognized the title because Momma Rose always said that it was one of her favorite movies. I not once guessed that it had been a book before it was a movie. And so many pages, I thought as I thumbed through it. Who would have known? The librarian had a strict rule that kids could only check out three books a person. Convinced that she might consider Gone with the Wind two books because of its sheer size, I placed two of the other books I had thought of checking out on a nearby shelf.

It was time to go. I knew that Nick was waiting. I hoped that Daisy had found what she was looking for and we could check out and leave. She was not in the Children's section. I whispered her name a few times but all I got was a dirty look from the librarian who pointed at the rolls of shelves I had just vacated.

I found Daisy sitting on the floor along the back wall in the corner looking at a picture book. Only she was not alone. Elvis sat beside her. He smiled a sly grin when he noticed me.

"Hello, pet. You missed a beautiful sky last night."

Shocked, I stiffened. "What are you doing here?"

My voice was louder because of the surprise and I got shushed from the librarian. Elvis got to his feet and dusted off his slacks. He dressed differently than most boys. Like today, for example, his pants were black and his shirt was pink. Pink?! What boy wears pink? Not that he looked girlie. No one would dare to say. Elvis had a manliness and swagger that couldn't be denied.

"That's some book you got there," he said.

"I like to read," I said defensively.

"You'd have to if you plan on reading whatever that is." He reached over and took it out of my hands and tested the weight of it. He looked at the title. "*Gone with the Wind*? No wonder that movie was so long."

"Have you seen it?"

"Yes, ma'am. It played in the theater where I use to work."

"You worked in a theater?" Daisy asked.

"I sure did. Best usher at the Loews State Theater."

I looked up at the clock. I knew we had to be leaving soon. I had a sneaking suspicion that Nick would hate to be kept waiting. Still, I wanted to speak to my new friend before rushing off.

"Daisy, why don't you take our books up to the desk? I'll give you my card to give the lady."

"Why?"

"So I can talk to Elvis for a minute."

"You know she won't let me check all of these out," Daisy said, holding up her books and then pointing to mine.

"Will you just go one up there?" I said.

She did as I asked but not without a few mumbled words on her way. I chose to ignore her. I turned my attention back to Elvis. "You really work at a theater?"

"I used to. It was a real sweet gig. I got to watch the movies and eat all the popcorn I could."

"Then why did you quit?" Sounded like a good deal if you asked me.

His cheeks turned red and he stumbled over his next words in embarrassment. "I didn't quit. You see there was this girl who worked behind the concession. She was the one who gave me the popcorn. I think she did it because she was sweet on me. I didn't encourage her none because my buddy liked her and all. I didn't see any problem in taking the popcorn."

"But your buddy did, didn't he?" I asked.

"Yes," Elvis's jaw tightened, "we ended up fighting right there in the lobby. The boss broke it up and fired both of us on the spot."

"And what happened to the girl? Did she still like you?"

"No, she called us both animals among a few other things. Last I heard she was dating the guy who replaced us."

"Ouch. I think Thelma is half in love with you because you did fight over her."

"That's nice, but it wasn't Thelma's hair he was pulling. You don't hit girls, kids, or my friends and that idiot was doing all three."

His words touched me profoundly. I felt something I rarely did. I felt protected in a way that was different from Momma Rose's gruff approach.

"So what types of books are you looking for?" I smiled.

"Not sure. I like biographies, I guess. I like to know what makes people tick. No *Duke and the Peasant Girl* for me," he gave me a teasing look.

"How..?" I blushed this time.

"She was reading it when I showed up."

I glanced around the shelves and toward the front desk.

He lifted a book off a nearby bookshelf and placed it back down. "I convinced her that she needed to read some books her own age."

"How did you do that?"

"I told her to and then we found her books she liked."

I was amazed. If I had suggested such a thing she would have caused a scene that would have gotten us kicked out. But Elvis? She ate right out of his hand. I looked up at the clock again. I really needed to leave.

"I have to go. Our ride is waiting."

"Then you better go. I wouldn't want you to get in trouble."

\*\*\*

I saw that Nick was put out as we approached the car. I hurriedly help Daisy into the back and got into the front seat.

"It's about time," Nick said, starting up the car, "I thought I told you to hurry?"

"Sorry," I mumbled hating that I felt the need to apologize. He did not have to volunteer to take us. The only reason he did was to gain favor with Momma Rose. I knew that.

Nick reached over and touched *Gone With the Wind*. "That's one hell of a book you got there."

I didn't say anything. Really what was there to say? It was a hell of a book, as he put it. Elvis said something similar. I defended myself then. Probably because I did not fear Elvis.

"I've never been much of a reader myself." His finger dropped from the book and hit the side of my thigh. He pulled his hand back and I told myself that it was an accident. There was nothing to it. Just awkward. Nick put both hands back on the wheel.

"I can't say that I ever wanted to be either. I barely made it through school."

Daisy was lost in her book and oblivious to anything around her. I wanted to know why he was sharing such a fact with me. It wasn't a fact to be proud of. I hoped he didn't tell Momma Rose that. She thought a lot of people with book learning. Even Daddy took a couple of trade school courses with the GI Bill.

We drove the rest of the way in silence. Once at the house I started to open the door when Nick touched my arm. He looked back at Daisy. "You go on inside, Daisy. I need to talk to your sister about something."

Once out of the car Daisy looked back at me. I tried to put her mind at ease. "Go. I'll be inside in a few minutes."

I could tell that she didn't want to go but did so because there was no other choice.

"I bet you are wondering why I've kept your secret from your mother."

"The thought has crossed my mind."

He pulled a pack of cigarettes out of his front pocket. I watched as he fired it up. The end of the cigarette glowed red. Nick puffed out a cloud of smoke that tickled my throat and made me want to vomit.

"I wanted to show you that we can keep things between us. There is no use bringing your mother in on a situation that's only going to hurt her in the end."

That seemed pretty reasonable to me. Hey, anything to keep me out of trouble sounded reasonable. "Okay."

"Now, I don't like you seeing that Elvis boy."

I geared up for Nick to tell me that I couldn't see Elvis anymore. That was not going to happen. I felt bad enough about standing him up the previous night. Nick took another drag and held it in for an extra second before exhaling through his nose. He resembled a fire eating dragon.

"I won't tell as long as you follow my orders. I mean it. No sass mouthing, no rolling your eyes when you think I'm not looking, none of that stuff. I ask you to do something and you do it. I say jump, you ask how high."

Nick must have seen qualities in me that I didn't even see. I would have done these things anyway. I feared authority, always had. I liked following the rules for the most part and despised getting into trouble. If you asked me, Thelma's the girl he needed to be having this conversation with.

Maybe it was a blessing that he saw those things. Like I said I don't rebel as a rule but I knew instinctively that I would for Elvis. Also for Jack. Not that it mattered because I knew that was a lost cause.

"I'm waiting on an answer, girl."

"I'll do it."

Nick grinned wolfishly. Wolfishly? Why did I keep comparing him to animals, even mystical creatures? "Good because we both know that you never really had a choice."

# CHAPTER FIFTEEN

The next few days went by pretty uneventfully. Which in kids' terms equals boring. We stayed close to the house. Except for Thelma. By the second night at home she was driving us all stir crazy. Daisy and I were happy when she finally snuck out the window to meet up with Eddie. I had hoped that she would return in a better state of mind.

Momma Rose was almost as bad. With her not having a night job about drove me batty as well. It wasn't as bad on the nights that Nick came over because he was the subject of her interest. We almost welcomed him just to get Momma's thoughts on someone else.

You see, when Momma Rose has too much time on her hands she feels compelled to fill it with other things. First it was the house. Once that was complete she started in on us girls. She decided to fix our flaws. Daisy's posture, my messiness, and don't even get started on Thelma.

Yes indeed, some nights I was happy to see Nick's face. We didn't talk much and never about our conversation in the car. It was odd that he rarely asked me to do anything for him. Granted, I did try and stay out of the way as much as possible.

Daisy on the other hand liked Nick. When he came over she was his shadow. It was like the bedtime debacle never happened. Oh, by the way, Daisy quizzed me on the parts of *The Duke and the Peasant Girl* she did read before Elvis got it away from her. Let me tell you that was a four hour conversation I never want to have again. She came up with some questions that I wanted to know the answers to as well. Our next visit to the library should prove educational as well as entertaining.

But back to Nick and Daisy. They shared jokes and played games. Always laughing and it seemed as if overnight I was no longer Daisy's best friend. I must admit it bothered me. Not a lot, but it did bother me. I confess I was the tiniest bit jealous.

Momma Rose smiled more often than I could remember in recent memory. At night after we had gone to bed was when she laughed. I don't know what Nick did or said but Momma Rose would laugh so loud that it would wake me up at two o'clock in the morning. Then there were the quiet nights. The nights that I didn't hear a whisper. It reminded me of nights spent with Daddy.

One of my very first memories was of Momma Rose and Daddy. I was about four years old. I woke up some time during the night and for some reason got out bed. I remember music playing in the background. One of Daddy's favorites, "Sunday Kind of Love". When it came on the radio he would stop and take Momma Rose in his arms.

That night was no different. I walked to the end of the hallway and stood there watching. The only lights came from a small end table lamp and from the streetlight outside. Daddy and Momma Rose were standing in the middle of the room. Momma Rose's head was laying against Daddy's shoulder. Daddy sang softly (and off-key) in her ear. They loved each other that night and for many nights after that. Then it all fell apart. Daddy left for Ohio and we ended up here.

It didn't seem fair but I guess life seldom is to people like us.

***

When I saw Elvis again it was early in the morning a couple days later. I had gotten up earlier than usual. The sunrise peeked over the horizon as I walked out on to the front steps for a change of scenery. The sun was pink in the morning sky and the streets were still quiet. It would be another half hour or so before the morning crowd began making their daily commute.

He came strolling up the sidewalk. His gray suit was wrinkled and looked slept in. His normally well-kept hair was a mess and he looked as if he hadn't slept in a week.

"Morning," I called out, running down to the edge of the sidewalk to meet him as he came up.

"Yeah, what is so good about it?"

"You're up pretty early. Or are you up pretty late?" I teased.

He kept walking. "I'm not in the mood today, pet. Tread very lightly."

I didn't. I knew he wasn't going to do anything to me so I began walking with him. "So where were you?"

"Out."

"That's all you are going to say?"

"That's all you need to know," he said curtly.

"So you aren't going to tell me?" I asked.

Elvis turned up the walk to his grandfather's house. "There's nothing to say."

And with that he walked inside and shut the door behind him. Something must have hurt him. Something or someone. I couldn't figure out which. I started to go home when the door opened again. I half-expected it to be J.D. but I was wrong. It was Elvis.

"You want to go for a walk?"

I shook my head. "Can't. Momma Rose hasn't left for work yet."

He looked around and motioned for me to follow him. On the other side of his house was a vacant home. The previous tenant had moved out in the middle of the night with no forwarding address and owing two months of rent. Elvis wanted to tell me something that he did not want others to overhear.

He settled with his back against the house and one foot lifted against it. His arms were folded against his chest and his look was bleak. I took a seat on a nearby tree stump. "What's going on?"

Elvis did his best not to fidget but I could tell that he was so upset he was about to bust. I just waited for the explosion to happen.

"I went down to the club last night. You see I met a guy who told me that this music producer was going to be there. I went there with the express purpose of talking to this creep. I wait there all night and you know what he does?"

"What?"

"Blows me off. Tells me that I'm just a kid and that I should just get a regular job like anyone else."

"Ouch," I said, for that stung even me. "Did he even listen to you?"

"That's just it. He said not to bother. Can you believe him?"

I could believe him. That was just it. I question Elvis's ability and I'm only eleven. This man, if he was who Elvis thought he was, dealt with people like Elvis every day.

"Have you ever thought about singing in one of these clubs you go to?"

Elvis calmed a bit. "Pet, it's not as easily as going up to one of these owner and asking to sing. It doesn't work like that."

"Why not?" I said. "If you are as good as you claim to be than that shouldn't be a problem."

I got him thinking on that one. "I know you're right, but…"

"But nothing," I said with the confidence of a person who had nothing to lose by the suggestion. "If you are as good as you say it will not be a problem."

"You still don't think I can sing. Can you?"

I shook my head. "You're probably good enough for church."

"Remind me to get my guitar and make you eat those words," he said.

"Anytime you want I'm ready."

"How about tonight? You think you could get out? You couldn't get into the club, of course, but we could meet out back. Closer to the alley."

Momma Rose was going out with Nick again. I doubted that she would be home before midnight. As long as I was in bed before they got back I should be fine. "I think we can do that. But it can't be as late. Say about ten?"

"It's a date," he said.

I watched as the tension in him lessened but did not completely evaporate. He reminded me of a cake timer about ready to go off. You know it's coming and you know what it sounds like but it still scares the crap out of you half the time. This once, I thought, I caught the timer before the alarm went off and managed to add more time. Next time would I be so lucky?

*** 

That evening I thought that I would never get away from Thelma. After we finished up dinner she kept waiting around the kitchen. I have no clue what she was waiting for but it seemed as if she wanted to ask me something. I was just about to ask her what was up when she went into the living room and turned the radio on. I guess she lost her nerve. After a few more minutes I heard her talking to Eddie. I went off to play with Daisy in Momma's room.

We were playing dress-up in Momma Rose's closet. I would have to make sure that everything made its way back to its place. Momma Rose had a fit if her things were out of order. We're not supposed to be in her room anyway. Daisy was standing in front of the mirror in a pair of black high heels and a hat with an attached veil.

"How do I look?" Daisy asked with a toothy grin. Did I tell you how hard it was to get mad at this child?

"Beautiful darling," I said in my best impression of a wealthy Upper East Side accent. I held out a bent wrist. On my arm were several bracelets and on my finger were two rings. It was all costume jewelry that Momma Rose had picked up at some garage sale or flea market.

The only real pieces she had were her engagement ring and a gold cross that had belonged to her grandmother. Two things that Momma Rose kept with her at all times. I don't think she ever took them off. I believe she even showered with them on. Momma said the jewelry was the only thing of worth that she owned and kept them with her to protect them. We had lived in many a place with shady characters. We also had to move out of a place swiftly sometimes and Momma Rose lived in fear of leaving valuables behind. I think that I get that from her. Granted no one wanted my picture of Daddy and bible but I lived in fear of losing either one. It was the only thing that I could compare it to.

Given it was summer, the sun had disappeared behind the horizon and the night had not reached full darkness when I went out to meet Elvis. Our backyard backed up to an alley that only the neighborhood people used. We had a wide iron gate that opened up to the street; if someone wanted they could pull a car into the yard. Elvis was on the other side of that gate, sitting on and wooden crate. In his arms was a guitar.

He strummed the strings with such care I knew it was his treasured possession. I didn't know the tune but it was a soft melody that called to me. So engrossed in the music I doubt that he even saw me. Then he opened his mouth and I was sold. I had never heard a voice like his before.

Elvis continued. His words telling me the story of a lost love. His voice convincing me of the hurt and betrayal in the song. I would never doubt him again. As he finished up I moved closer. He didn't look up at me until a few seconds after he was done.

"Well, pet. What do you think?" The twinkle in his eye and the smile on his lips said he already knew the answer.

"Are you serious?" I asked. "That was fantastic!"

He blushed and looked away. "I could practice that chorus some more. You know, even out the rough edges."

"I think it is perfect just as it is."

He liked hearing that. Not that he said it. It was in the relief of his shoulders and the smile on his face. "So what should I do next? About the agent I mean?"

The fact that he was asking advice from an eleven-year-old did not seem odd to either of us. "I think that you need to forget about an agent and play."

"I was thinking that when I went back to Memphis I could cut a record. There is this record studio not real far from my house that I could try. The guy who runs it, Sam, he likes a lot of the same music that I do and I think that it would be a good fit."

"Sounds like a plan."

"I figure I got to do something. I want to make a go of this music thing."

"What if it doesn't work? I mean what will you do then?" I asked.

His hand patted the guitar. Almost as if he was stroking it. "I figure if it doesn't work it's not meant to be. I can be happy driving a truck the rest of my life but only if I know that I tried. You get what I'm saying, pet?"

The funny thing was I did. "The only failure is not trying."

"Exactly," he grinned at me. I listened as Elvis played a few more songs. Mostly they were covers of popular songs. Each one was better than the next. He then played something he called rhythm and blues. My music education grew by the minute. I had never heard music like this on the radio. The radio was filled with bubblegum tunes, country and big band swing. Not this music that lived and breathed. Beats that called to one's soul. I was instantly hooked.

I knew next to nothing about music. I listened, but did not really hear until this night. I asked as many questions that I could and Elvis did his best to explain the answers to me. Time completely escaped me and the next thing I knew headlights were pulling in to the driveway.

"Crap," I said, getting up from the ground. "I've got to go. Momma Rose finds me outside with another boy she will skin me alive."

"Another boy?" Elvis asked. "What other boy?"

I heard a door shut. I looked toward the house and back to Elvis. "I'll explain later. 'Bye."

I thought I heard him chuckle as I ran off but I will never be sure.

## CHAPTER SIXTEEN

I guess you are wondering if I made it back into the house unseen. I did. I beat Momma Rose by a clear minute. I grabbed a glass out of the cupboard and went to the refrigerator and poured me a glass, spilling about half of it on the table. I was wiping up the mess when Momma Rose came into the room.

"Oh, May," Momma Rose said, looking back over her shoulder, "I thought you girls were in bed."

I held up my glass. "I couldn't sleep and thought this might help."

"We-well," Momma Rose said with another look behind her.

"Momma are you okay?" I asked, concerned.

"Yes, I'm fine," she said, twirling her engagement ring around her finger.

"Are you sure?"

"Yes, May. I'm fine. I'm going to bed. You finish that glass and get to bed. You hear me?"

"Yes ma'am." I said, happy that she was going to let it go at that. My story of sleeplessness would fail to hold up under more questioning. I finished the milk and turned off the light. I had got away with one tonight, but guessing by Momma Rose's reaction maybe she had gotten away with something as well.

\*\*\*

At six-thirty my eyes popped open. I threw my legs over the side of the bed and sat up. Thelma and Daisy were both sound asleep so I did my best to tiptoe around the room so not to bother them.

After my morning pee, I went to the kitchen in search of breakfast. When I opened the door I found out I wasn't alone. Sitting there at the table dressed only in his blue jeans and white undershirt was Nick.

"Morning," he said, looking up from the paper. I'm guessing that he got it from his own porch or even went down to the corner market to get it since Momma Rose refused to pay for the news.

"Good morning," I said, debating going back to my room. I figured it would be rude so I stayed. Had Nick spent the night last night? Suddenly Momma Rose's behavior all made sense. Nick had been with her when she came into the kitchen the previous night. She was nervous that I would see him and guess what they were doing. Which was exactly what they were doing.

"Your Momma went to work early."

"Did she?" I said, hoping I didn't sound as freaked out as I felt, "I didn't know."

I heard him ruffle the paper behind me. *Come on Thelma, Daisy, please wake up.*

"You remember how I told you I could keep a secret?"

My stomach began to roll over on itself. This could not be good. I turned to face Nick. "Yes."

He placed the paper on the table and intertwined his fingers on top of it. "I told your Momma that I would go home before you girls woke up."

"I won't tell her."

He stood up and came around the table, pinning me between him and the counter. "That's not the only secret you'll need to keep."

"Okay. What else?"

He wiggled his index finger at me. "Not so fast. I thought I told you that I didn't like that Presley boy. And then I see you with him again last night."

"How?" I asked in disbelief. There was no way.

"It doesn't matter. Just know that I did."

I tried another tactic.

"You didn't say I couldn't see him. Besides we weren't doing anything."

"True, but there is only one thing a boy his age wants out of a young girl like you. Sex."

No one in my entire life had been that blunt about the subject. I was surprised to say the least. I was even more surprised when Nick touched my shoulder. I pushed closer to the counter but it did not do any good. Warning bells were going off in my head.

"What are you doing?"

Nick stepped closer, his body pressing against me. His hand dropped to my breast, cupping it through my shirt. "I'm showing you what boys like Presley want." And just like that he pulled away and went back around the table. His voice so matter of fact that I thought maybe I had dreamed it up.

"They'll hurt you, May. If you will let him, he will make you into a whore. I'm going to make damn sure that doesn't happen."

I did not waste any time. I walked as fast as my feet would carry me back into my bedroom. I locked the door and threw myself onto the bed and under the covers. My back to the door as if I could block Nick out as long as I didn't see him. My body trembled as I thought about what happened. My entire world seemed to turn on its axis.

He said that he was teaching me a lesson. That boys only wanted one thing out of me. My heart told me that Nick had no clue about Elvis. I knew that Elvis saw me as a friend and nothing else. He had never done anything to indicate otherwise. Nick was the one who was wrong.

I played the entire scene over and over again. I did not understand why Nick had touched me. The teach-me-a-lesson thing seemed like a lie. But if he was out to hurt me, why did he leave it at that? Only one touch when he could have done so much more?

I debated telling Momma Rose. She would surely know what to do. But I had that nagging doubt. What if she thought it was my fault? She liked Nick enough to have him stay over at the house. What if she believed his version of events or worse yet, called me a liar?

No, I decided, I couldn't tell Momma Rose. I couldn't tell anyone. I was not willing to take the chance that they didn't believe me. It was a secret and one that my shame was willing to keep. The tears did not come that day. I was too afraid to let them fall.

I stayed in bed much of the day. I dozed off and on but mainly I just laid in my bed trying my best to think of nothing. When Thelma grew worried (I'm notorious for never lying about) she brought me in some lunch. One of my favorites, grilled cheese and tomato soup. My stomach, remembering that I had skipped breakfast, growled. I sat up and ate while a worried Thelma felt my cheeks for a fever.

"Cool as a cucumber," she said, baffled.

"I'm fine," I mumbled between bites.

"Well, just the same I told Daisy to stay outside and play until we knew for sure."

"Who is with her?"

"Nick's across the street. Apparently he didn't go to work today but I asked Vera to keep an eye on her," Thelma said. "She's been working out in the yard all day."

I relaxed and took another bit of my sandwich. "That's nice of her but I'm fine. Really."

"Then you want to tell me what is going on?"

I shook my head. "There's nothing."

Thelma placed her hands on her hips. She looked less like a wild cousin/ big sister and more like a momma bear trying to protect one of her cubs. "I don't believe you."

I hated to keep this secret from Thelma. It weighted down on my shoulders and threatened to drown me. I knew that if I unburdened myself that not only would I risk denial, I would place the weight onto my cousin's. It was my burden and was not fair to Thelma.

"I'll be okay. I promise you, Thelma. Please don't pressure me anymore on this, will ya?"

Thelma deliberated the request for a moment. When she opened her mouth to answer I prepared for her to say more than she did. Instead she gave me a one word response.

"Okay."

I could see that it was taking everything in her to let the subject go. For now at least. And for now was all I needed.

# CHAPTER SEVENTEEN

We ate supper again as a family that night. Nick and Daisy teased and joked as they set the table. Momma Rose fixed pork chops and potatoes that Nick brought over, giving us a break from our beans routine. Momma went on and on how nice it was to fix something different. If this morning had not have happened I probably would have chirped the same tune as well.

Only it had happened. Sitting at the table from Nick I watched for signs that he acknowledged or even remembered. He barely even spoke to me, instead focusing all of his attention on Momma and Daisy. Not that it was a big surprise. Thelma and I always seemed to be thought of last.

"What's wrong with you?" Momma Rose said, noting that I was picking at my dinner.

"Nothing," I said.

"She's been like this all day," Thelma said. "I took her temperature and she was fine."

"I am fine," I said, growing annoyed.

"I don't know. You don't look sick," Momma Rose said concerned. "Is something hurting you?"

I hated all of the attention. "Nothing's hurting Momma."

"You promise?"

"I promise," I said, crossing my fingers underneath the table because I was lying. My head and heart were hurting.

"You heard the girl," Nick finally joined the conversation, "she's fine. Now quit making such a fuss over her."

And like that it was over. Because Nick, sitting at the head of the table like a king on his throne, deemed it so. I was both happy and mad. My feelings were so out of control. Tears stung my eyes for the first time that day. I looked down at my plate and quickly blinked them away.

Momma Rose looked at me strangely again when, after dessert, I volunteered to do the dishes even though it was Thelma's turn. Thelma, on the other hand, had no qualms about it. She had a legitimate date with Eddie that night and was in a hurry to start getting ready. The other three went out on the front porch to sit and talk.

I carried all of the dishes into the kitchen before running hot water in the sink. With the exception of the record player playing in the bedroom the house was pretty quiet. I got lost in my thoughts about Jack as I washed. I thought about where he was and what I could do to change his mind. I also could not keep my mind from thinking about what Nick said. Would Jack only want that from me? Or would he want more?

Nick interrupted my train of thought. "I'll be back in a minute. I'm just going to get me a glass of water."

I stopped what I was doing and grabbed a towel to dry off my hands. The closer Nick got, the more the panic in me started to grow. "I'll just get out of your way."

He laughed when I turned to face him and realized that he had me cornered against the cabinets. How did he keep doing that? I moved a few steps to the right and into the corner of the countertop. Nick got a cup out of the sink and turned on the tap.

I watched as he filled the glass. The clear liquid threatened to overflow the rim of the glass. Nick lifted the glass to his lips and I watched his throat as he swallowed the water in three gulps. When he finished he filled it again and set it to the counter beside me.

"I didn't mean to scare you this morning," Nick said.

"You didn't scare me," I said. "I'm fine."

"You've said your fine about a dozen times in the last hour and none of us believe you."

He told the truth. None of them believed me and he was the only one who knew why. I bit my lower lip. How did I get out of this one?

"May, you are a pretty girl. Probably one of the prettiest girls this block has ever seen."

If I had the room I would be pacing. Since I didn't, I rubbed the palms of my hands up and down my sides. My lungs seemed to struggle for air and my heart felt as if it would explode at any second.

In an attempt to get away I stepped forward. Nick caught my arm. "I was paying you a compliment."

"Thank you," I said. "Now excuse me—"

He pushed me back and my hip hit the counter. A burning sensation went down the side of my leg. I tried to keep from shouting but a moan escaped my lips. I turned my body toward the counter on instinct and Nick came up behind me.

"Everything alright in there?" came Momma Rose's voice.

Nick wrapped an arm around my chest and upper arms.

"We're fine," Nick said, sounding as natural as I had ever heard him. "Clumsy here hit her hip on the cabinet."

"Tell her you are fine," he whispered in my ear.

"I'm good," I called out in a surprisingly calm voice.

Momma Rose didn't say anything else.

"Good girl," Nick's lips were against my neck, "this is just between us. Do you understand?"

I nodded.

"Good because your momma won't believe you and it would just devastate Daisy. I would hate to hurt that little girl but I will. You just keep doing what I tell you to do and everybody will be happy."

"And if I don't?"

"You don't want to know."

Not needing anymore reassurances Nick let me go. He slapped me on the butt. "Now finish those dishes, girl."

I moved back in front of the sink. My thoughts racing, tears filling my eyes. What kind of funhouse had I just entered and more importantly how did I get my family out of it in one piece?

I wiped away an angry tear. Tears would not help me now. I needed to figure out a way to break up Momma Rose and Nick. I had no ideas and really no hope. Then I thought of Elvis. Maybe he could help me. I wouldn't tell him about Nick, of course, but maybe he would help me anyhow. It was worth a shot.

Maybe the only shot I had left.

\*\*\*

The next days after that night were a bit of a blur. I didn't see Nick again that week. Both he and Momma Rose went out or she stayed at home alone with us girls. Things went back to the way they had been for the most part. The only changes I found were within myself. I found myself questioning everything and every person in my life. Even Daisy.

Momma Rose knew something was wrong. She didn't say anything but I knew she knew. I would catch her looking at me with her brows all wrinkled together and a frown on her face. She looked at me like I was some sort of math problem that she could not solve. I tried to pretend I didn't notice. Hell, I tried to pretend that nothing after Nick had happened. Only they made it impossible to do so. Daisy's constant chatter about how great Nick was and Momma Rose's soft smiles when his name was mention made me want to puke.

I didn't make my mornings with J.D. I frequently slept to mid-morning or later. One day, Thursday I think, I slept until three in the afternoon. I got up long enough to use the bathroom, shower, pick at my dinner, and then went back to bed and slept another ten hours.

My day of sleep must have scared both Momma Rose and Thelma because when I woke up Friday (at nine a.m.) they were both waiting for me at the kitchen table.

"Sit down May Louise."

*Louise*, I thought. Anytime a child hears their middle name they instantly know they are in trouble. I had not done much in the last few days so I didn't fear getting in trouble. I took a seat next to Thelma.

"May, this has got to stop," Momma Rose said, speaking first.

"What's got to stop Momma?" I asked.

"This moodiness. Sleeping all the time. Acting like you don't care about anything."

"It's scaring us May," Thelma added.

"I'm not trying to scare anyone. I'm not trying to do anything," I said.

Momma Rose reached across the table and took my hand. "I know that, sweetie. If I thought you were, this conversation would be going another way." Momma took a deep breath. "I've been talking with Nick and he seems to think that you are mooning over that boy I caught you with."

Jack had been so far from my mind the drive-in felt like it was a hundred years and not just six days prior. Nick was giving a reason that threw Momma Rose off the scent. I knew instinctively he wanted me to go along with it but I couldn't. "It's not Jack."

"Jack," Momma Rose said his name like she was banking the name for future reference.

"Then if it isn't him, what is it?"

I lifted my shoulders. "I don't know. Maybe those teenage hormones are kicking in already."

"Is it your period?" Thelma asked.

"Thelma," Momma Rose admonished.

Thelma held up her hands. "I'm just asking. We both know how it can be. Maybe May's going to be like this once a month."

"It's not my period," I said. In truth it was a fair question. I had only started getting my period in April. I realized after saying that it wasn't my period it was the perfect excuse. Momma Rose hated talking about all bodily functions. I could have said it was that and she would have let the discussion go.

"Well I don't know what it is then, but it's going to stop. You hear me?" Momma Rose said, agitated. "It's not fair that we have to walk on egg shells around you."

"How did this get to be my fault? I haven't done anything," I said, my voice an octave higher than normal.

"You're making me feel bad and I don't like it. Is this about me seeing Nick?"

"What? No."

"It is, isn't it?" Momma Rose said, getting out of her chair, "He said that you didn't like him and I told him he was being crazy."

"I don't like him," I said.

Momma Rose looked at me, her hands on her hips and a defiant look in her eye. "Well you better learn to like him because he ain't going nowhere. You hear me, little girl? I'm happy for the first time since your sorry ass daddy came into my life. I'm not about to let you screw that up for me."

"Aunt Rose," Thelma said, a bit astonished herself, "That's not what we planned."

"That's when I thought it was about that stupid boy. You want to take her shopping it's on you."

We watched Momma Rose as she got her purse and headed out the door. She called for Daisy and after a moment I heard a car start up. I looked to Thelma.

"Nick, gave her one of his old cars."

"He's really tied himself to this family hasn't he?" My question was rhetorical but Thelma answered anyway.

"Yes he has, and I don't see Aunt Rose leaving him."

"We will just have to break them up."

Thelma slumped back into her seat. "It would have been a lot easier if we had done it before they started playing hide the salami."

"Hide the what?"

"Before he started staying the night."

"Oh." That I got. "There has to be a way."

"I don't see how. It looks like Nick's in it for the long haul."

I had a dream the night before. It was a vision of the future. A bleak future. Nick and Momma Rose getting married. A small church wedding with only a few of us in attendance. Thelma, Daisy, and I would wear matching dressings and walking down the aisle as bridesmaids. Nick would watch as I made my way. He wouldn't say a word. He would just lift a finger to his lips.

It wasn't one of those dreams that you wake up from and go back to sleep. It was a dream that went on and on. I shuddered. Nick and I were suddenly alone in a bedroom and he had a right to me because I was his wife. His wife. It got more disturbing after that but I'm done talking about it for now.

"So what did Momma Rose mean when she mentioned shopping?"

"Oh, she thought that if we went and did a little shopping that you might get out of your mood."

"But I hate shopping."

Thelma nodded. "We were grasping at straws. We wanted you to be May again."

I wanted to tell her that I would never be that May again. Even if I shopped for a million years. "So what are we going to do now?"

"We could go to the library."

I shook my head.

"Well shopping's out," Thelma said, biting her lip.

"Yes."

Thelma thought about it and she said up as if she had a brilliant idea. "I've got it. You go get changed. We are going to get you a makeover."

"A makeover?"

"Yeah," Thelma's eye lit up as she explained, "I've got some friends down at the trade school that are always looking for models to practice on. We will go down there get your hair done, a nice polish on the nails, and then have lunch at Woolworth's."

While the idea intrigued me I didn't know if it was a good idea. Momma Rose was already mad enough at me. "What if one of them turns my hair blue or something?"

"That's not going to happen. Besides, I wouldn't let them dye your hair."

I wasn't completely sold on the idea. "What are we going to do for money?"

"You let me worry about that." Then, not giving me any time to think, Thelma grabbed my hand and pulled me to my feet. "You won't regret it."

I knew that I would possibly regret it. I also knew that I was going to do it anyway. You want to know why? Because Momma Rose would have hated it. Had she been there she would have forbidden it. *Well,* I decided, *she's not here and I'm going to have a little fun.*

# CHAPTER EIGHTEEN

The girls at the trade school were all very nice. Thelma knew more than one of them and when we came in the front door they all stopped what they were doing and came forward to speak to us. Thelma told the girl, Judy, who was to work on my hair, that I wanted to looked like Elizabeth Taylor. I told Judy as she began cutting that I knew that she wasn't a miracle worker and just to do the best she could with my long and stringy mess. I also told her when Thelma wasn't listening that I wanted it to touch my shoulders and go no higher.

After Judy got done cutting (which took forever since she was adding what she called layers to it) Thelma and I got our nails done. Since my hair was not fixed they would not let me look at it. So my back was to the mirror as I was led over to the manicurist station.

Thelma picked out a fire engine red for her color. I stuck with pink. More of a pastel pink and not the hot pink Thelma wanted me to pick. The hot pink just wasn't me. The girls chattered and gossiped while our nails finished drying. I heard enough about boys to not only educate me but to make me blush.

It was the most fun I had in a long time. When my nails were done I was led back to the chair (again I couldn't look in the mirror). Judy dried my hair and then she brushed and curled and used an aerosol setting spray (her fancy words for hairspray). Then she brushed and curled some more. By the time she was done my lungs were begging for mercy.

Thelma beamed with excitement beside my chair as I was swiveled around. All I can say is wow, Judy must be some type of miracle worker after all. I didn't look like Elizabeth Taylor, but really who did? I ran my finger over my hair. My hair was indeed short. The curvy waves framed my face and I looked…grown up.

"You sure do," Thelma said.

I must have said the words out loud given that Thelma answered.

"Let's put some makeup on her," one of the girls said.

"She can be like a real, live dress up doll," another chimed in.

Thelma stepped between me and the makeup mafia. "No makeup. Aunt Rose is probably going to kill me and her both now."

I thanked Judy and the others for all that they had done for me and followed Thelma out of the salon. We ran across the street and began our walk to Woolworth's. It was a much slower walk than it normally would be since I stopped ever few windows to look at my hair.

"Do you really think Momma Rose will hate it?" I said, stopping to look in a toy store's window.

"I'm willing to bet she will. You know how she is May. She hates everything she doesn't think of first. Cutting your hair would be one of the last things she would think about doing."

"Well I like it."

Thelma smiled. "I like it too."

We got to the lunch counter and ordered our meal. A grilled cheese for me. Thelma got a hamburger. We both ordered fries and a coke. We got about halfway through the meal when Thelma asked me, "May, you like Eddie don't you?"

"He's okay."

Thelma put her hamburger down and picked up her napkin. She dabbed the corners of her mouth. "But do you like him?"

"Eddie's Eddie. I don't dislike him. Why?" I asked.

"No reason. It's just that I like Eddie a lot and he likes me."

We all knew Eddie was crazy in love with Thelma. Until now I thought she was lukewarm on him at best. I could see that wasn't the case. "Eddie loves you Thelma."

"I know." She grinned and for probably the first time in her life resembled humble, "I know."

"Well what's all this talk about?"

"You sounded just like Aunt Rose there."

I didn't think so and rolled my eyes at her. "I just want you to get on with whatever it is you are trying to tell me."

Now that did sound like Momma.

Hemming and hawing wasn't Thelma's style and the more she did it the more it worried me. What if I didn't like what she was about to say? What if it changed everything? What if? What if? What if?

"Eddie wants me to marry him."

The other shoe dropped and it fell right on my head. I have to admit I didn't handle it too well either. More Momma Rose came spilling out of my mouth than May Louise Richards did. "What do you mean he asked you to marry him? Is he crazy?"

"May," Thelma said, looking around, "lower your voice will you? I don't want the entire city of Louisville knowing my business."

"You can't marry him. You're only sixteen."

"My granny was only thirteen when she married my papaw and they've been married thirty-seven years."

"They got married back in the dark ages. People don't have to do that now."

We both began eating again. Thelma upset that I wasn't happy about her proposal. Me, I was mad. I knew that Thelma and Eddie would get hitched someday. That did not bother me. What bothered me was I felt that she was abandoning me just when I needed her the most. When I needed an ally against Nick.

*I could tell her what happened*, I thought before dismissing the idea. She may not believe me. What could be worse was if she did believe me. What then? Nick had not mentioned Thelma when he threatened me but knowing this might just put her in danger.

We did not have to wait to pay for lunch after eating. Woolworth's had a rash of kids doing what is known as dine and dash. That's where you order your food, eat, and then leave without paying. Our waitress was a smart one who insisted we pay before she would bring us the meal. Not that we would have done that. I'm just saying that if I was eyeing us I would be a little cautious as well.

My moods had felt like they had been on the tilt-a-whirl today. Up, down, and all around. If this was what being a teenager was like I prayed for my twenties to come fast. It was all Nick's fault. Knowing it didn't make it any easier to handle. Made it worse because it gave me someone other than myself to blame.

We wandered through the racks of clothes, each lost in our own little worlds. I was about to give up and wait outside when I saw something moving inside one of the rounders. I stepped in for a closer look when I saw a hand reach up and remove a shirt from a hanger.

*A thief.* I thought of marching off in the opposite direction. The last thing I needed was for store security to think that I was in o it. The rounder began moving again. This time I saw a body. A boy's head and shoulders emerged and stood up. He glanced around, I guess to see who was watching.

It was Jack.

"Hey," he said, batting away a lock of blond hair that had fallen over his eyes.

I could see he was holding a bag behind his back. "Hi."

"You look different."

"Thelma and I got my hair done," I said. "What are you doing?"

"Just doing a little shopping."

"Inside the clothes rounder?"

He put his hand on the metal rack. "Is that what they call it?"

I nodded. "Thelma use to work at the one across town last summer before she got fired."

"What did she get fired for?"

"Being late mostly but mainly because the owner's husband was sweet on her."

Jack relaxed a little. I decided not to bring the bag up. We all have out issues I guess. If he wanted to talk about it we would. I also decided that if he carried that bag toward the door it didn't matter how much I wanted to go with him. He would be on his own.

"I wonder what she's going to do when she and Eddie get married?" he asked.

"You know about that?" I asked.

"Yep, Eddie told me a couple of days ago that he was going to ask her," Jack said, "From the looks of it you aren't too happy about it."

I frowned. "I'm not."

"Why not?"

"I don't care to talk about it."

"Well what do you want to talk about?"

I looked down at the ground. Jack was in my line of sight and I saw his tennis shoes. They were old and dirty but I didn't pay no mind to that. My play shoes looked just as bad. What I saw was the seam that was coming undone. A bit of silver tape was holding it together.

"You need some new shoes."

He hid his foot behind his other shoe. "My good ones are at home. I didn't want to get them dirty while at the pool today."

I bit my lip. I knew that other kids were poorer than Daisy and me. Momma Rose made sure of that. I hated thinking of Jack with a hole in his shoe. But Thelma told me that men were prideful and did not want pity from anyone. Especially a girl.

Jack eyed one of the sales girls folding shirts at a nearby table. "I better be going now."

"Why? You...we haven't even discussed the drive-in."

"Oh." Jack rubbed the back of his neck. "I've forgotten all about that."

"But I lied," I said, ready to throw myself on the mercy of the court.

"I wasn't mad about that."

"You weren't?"

He had a wonderful smile. When he turned that smile and piercing blue eyes on me I was mush. He leaned in (only I didn't mind it when Jack did it) and said, "I already knew how old you were. Besides a year isn't all that long."

"Then what were you mad at?"

"Not what. Who. I was mad at your mom. She treated me like I was a piece of dirt. I may be poor but I'm not dirt."

At his raised voice the sales girl glanced at us again. Jack didn't see it though, he had brought the bag into view. He looked long and hard at it. I could see that he was battling some inner battle that I was not privy to. I held my hand out to him. Not because I wanted the bag but because I wanted to help him make a better choice.

When he let the bag fall to the floor and took my hand I let out a breath I had not been aware that I was holding. There were going to be more talks about more things. But it was enough for now that he held my hand.

I guess we all have our demons.

# CHAPTER NINETEEN

Jack and I waited outside until Thelma finished shopping. Jack and I said our goodbyes and he left us standing there in front of Woolworth's. We avoided talking about Eddie. Instead she quizzed me on Jack. Then when it was my turn and I asked her some questions of my own, she refused to answer them. She said that it was not fair for me to know so much about him. That if I wanted to know then I should ask him the questions myself.

I told her that was what I was going to do the next time I saw him. Which I hoped to be at the drive-in on Saturday. I had my doubts about that considering how mad Momma Rose was when she left this morning. I'm guessing my hair ain't going to make things any better.

Walking into the house that evening I felt like Marie Antoinette making her way to the guillotine. All I need was a lone drummer banging on a drum. The house was quiet. It gave me a little bit of hope that maybe Momma was taking a nap or was still out. The second one was a stretch to believe. The new to Momma Rose car sat empty in the driveway. Thelma gave my hand a little squeeze and looked me in the eyes. She wasn't going to leave me alone in this. I took a few deep breaths and then jerked my head.

"Aunt Rose? Daisy? We're home," Thelma shouted out to the house. I did not hear anything. Then there was a pattering of feet.

"Rose? Daisy?" Thelma called out again, "Where are you guys?"

I heard a door open. Daisy came down the hall. "I'm mad at you."

"Why?" Thelma asked, throwing herself down on the couch.

"Because you left me with Momma Rose all day. She was mad at you and took it out on me."

"Where is she now?" There was no way Daisy speaks so freely with Momma Rose in the house.

"She's over at Nick's. He called and asked Momma Rose to come over. She told me to come and knock on the door when you two got here."

"You mean to tell me Momma Rose left you alone?" I asked in disbelief.

Daisy nodded. "I'm not a baby. I can take care of myself."

We all knew that was not the case. I thought better of saying it though. If I did I knew I would spend the next hour having a childish argument about whether or not Daisy was grown or not. I've got enough wars to wage to add a petty battle with Daisy.

What I had was a huge problem with was the fact Daisy got left alone so that Momma Rose could go be with Nick. That was so not like her. Momma Rose always thought of Daisy and me first and now with Nick it seemed that she put herself at the top of the list.

"I better go get her," Daisy said.

"You go right there and right back," I said. "Don't dawdle."

After Daisy went out the door I looked up at that clock. Six p.m. Supper time usually and there were no signs that Momma Rose had even considered what we were having let alone began cooking.

"She's acting like a teenager with her first crush," Thelma said as if she was reading my thoughts. "She's only thinking of herself."

I didn't say anything. Instead I picked up a glass and plate that Momma had been using as an ashtray. From looking at the cigarette butts I knew they were not Momma's. Not her brand and they had all been smoked down to the filter. They had to be Nick's.

As I was emptying the plate in the garbage can the door opened. Daisy came in first followed by Momma Rose. She looked pretty much as she had this morning only a bit more calm. Not calm serene. No, Momma Rose looked the calm you get right before a tornado comes to town.

I turned and waited. I looked her straight in the eye. Not scared. Not defiant. I was just waiting to see. She nodded her head at me. "Tell me this wasn't your idea?"

My hair. "I like it."

"It's my fault Aunt Rose. I suggested we go down to the trade school and get our hair done." Thelma got up and came over to me. She linked her arm though mine. "Isn't she just beautiful? I think she looks like Elizabeth Taylor."

"I liked it longer," Momma Rose said, "but it will grow back out."

"I like your fingers," Daisy said.

"Aren't they pretty?" I said, holding one hand out so that we could both admire them.

Momma Rose held out her own hand. She had red polish on them but not as neat as mine was. She had put the color on herself a few nights before. "Now these are pretty hands. They work hard to take care of you."

I really saw Momma's hands with that comment. The cuticles were rough. There were a few burn scars from getting too close to the fryer at work. I realized that it was Momma Rose that needed the manicure more than me.

"Maybe next time we can go together," I offered. "They don't charge anything to do it."

"Maybe," Momma Rose said in that way she does when she doesn't want to do something. "We'll see. Now won't you girls go get cleaned up and then come help me with dinner."

And that was it. There was not yelling about my hair. There was nothing said about the cross words of this morning. We all just acted as if this morning never happened at all. Isn't that funny? Family's work in weird ways. They say that every family is different and I believe them because I have never seen a family like mine. We somehow work when it looks as if it should all fall apart.

\*\*\*

At dinner that night Momma Rose told us that she had gotten a second job cleaning an office at the car lot down the road. She seemed pretty excited about it; well, as excited as anyone could get about getting a job cleaning an office. Apparently Nick was friends with the owner and he put in a good word for Momma Rose.

I could not help but breathe a sigh of relief. With Momma Rose working four nights a week she would not have a lot of time for Nick. Maybe that would be enough to break them up. Thelma and I talked about it later that night. Thelma did not have as much hope as I did in the matter. She said she knew lust and Momma Rose had a bad case of it.

I had hope. It was all I had if I was to get away from Nick.

The next morning J.D. was standing at the fence when I came out onto the porch. "Girl, you want to tell me where in the sam hell you have been? I've been worried sick over you."

That made me smile. This little old man watching out for me. It was nice to feel looked after after the last few days. "I'm sorry J.D. I've been a little sick lately."

He looked me over from head to toe.

"You do look a little peaked. I got so worried I almost stopped your Momma yesterday morning. The only thing that stopped me was her stomping out to the car looking as mad as the devil."

"I'm glad you didn't. I was the reason Momma was so mad yesterday."

He started to say something else but I cut him off before he could ask anymore. Momma Rose would hate to think that the neighbors were gossiping about her. "It's all fine now. It was mother and daughter stuff."

"If you say so," he said. "I wouldn't know anything about that."

"No I guess you wouldn't. How's Elvis doing?"

"He's fine," J.D. said. "Last couple of days all he has done is fiddle with that guitar. He's not half bad, you know?"

"I know," I smiled at him, "he's good."

"I hope he doesn't think he can make a living at it though," J.D. said and then shook his paper at me. "Well I better get to it. I wanted to make sure you were okay before I did."

"I'm fine." There was that word again. I have said it a lot recently.

J.D. turned and started to walk away. I stopped him.

"Hey J.D.?"

"Yes?"

"Will you tell Elvis that I think the stars will be shining at eleven tonight?"

"What? What in the hell is that supposed to mean?" he asked

"Just tell him, he'll understand."

I needed to talk to Elvis. The longer I waited to figure out how to break up Momma Rose and Nick the closer Nick got to what he wanted out of all of us.

"So will you?"

J.D. gave me a curt nod. I knew he did not understand my request but with that nod I felt like he got it was code. I suddenly felt like we were government spies working on a mission. First Marie Antoinette, now spies. I guess my reading has broadened my imagination. I could only hope that it gave me the smarts to deal with the nemesis of my own story.

## CHAPTER TWENTY

Elvis showed up at five minutes to eleven. With Momma Rose working nights again and Thelma chatting on the phone with Eddie it was almost too easy to get away. Even Nick, according to Momma Rose, was having the boys over for poker. After making sure that Daisy was good and asleep I snuck out the window. I was careful to look around for any prying eyes. Not seeing any, I made my way through the backyard and let myself out of the gate.

When Elvis showed up I held a finger to my mouth to keep him from greeting me. I motioned for him to follow me and we had walked two blocks before I broke our silence.

"I wasn't sure you would meet me."

"Why not, pet?"

"I didn't know if J.D. would give you the message."

He walked with his hands clasped behind his back. "He's good for some things. Though he did want me to elaborate on what it meant."

"What did you tell him?"

"That it was none of his business. So why the silence?"

I knew I would have to explain that and had my answer ready. "My mother is dating our neighbor across the street."

"The guy with the cars in the yard?"

I nodded. "His name is Nick. The first night you and I went for a walk he saw us."

"And he told your momma?" he asked.

"Not exactly. Let's just say I would rather him not knowing about us meeting again."

Elvis stopped in his tracks. "We've done nothing to be ashamed of. You're just a girl. I've been completely honorable."

"Oh, I know that. He threatened me with it."

"Threatened you?"

We came upon the neighborhood park that Daisy and I visited on occasion. I knew that there was a park bench near the swings. When we got there we both settled in for a chat.

"He's using it as leverage against me. Momma Rose would hit the roof if she knew I was sneaking out of the house and meeting a boy. Any boy."

"I don't doubt that. What kind of leverage are you talking about?"

"He wants me to behave and do exactly what he tells me to do. I think he's afraid that I will make waves with him and Momma Rose."

Elvis nodded. "And do you, pet?"

"Do I what? Want to make waves?" I asked.

He nodded.

"I didn't at first but now I do," I did not say anymore fearing that I would give myself away. "But I need your help to do it."

"Me?" He half laughed. "What do you want me to do?"

"That's just it. I need help figuring it out. I don't know what to do."

"So let me get this straight. You want to break your Momma and this guy up? A man that I suppose she likes. You have no plan on how to do it and he has dirt on you that would get you in trouble? Am I clear?"

Hearing it put like that I knew it sounded as hopeless as I felt. No way in the world would Elvis help me. I could not blame him. I was asking for him to accept a fool's mission. There was a high potentiality it would all blow up in my face. If Elvis was associated with any plan he would be in as much trouble as I was.

"I guess it's kind of stupid."

"Not stupid, just not well thought out. We will have to work on this. Can you give me a couple of days to figure it out?"

I agreed but I knew that he was just being nice to me. There was no good plan to be had. I felt on my own. Again. Would this feeling ever go away? I decided to change the subject. "So where are you off to tonight? You don't look dressed up enough to go to a club."

"I've got a date," Elvis said and even in the moonlight I could see a crimson blush stain his cheek.

"This late at night?"

"She's a waitress over at the Nightingale and doesn't get off work until midnight. I told her that I would meet her and made sure she got home okay."

At eleven I did not know what or where The Nightingale was. I did know at eleven that most dates consisted of more than a walk home. "What's her name?"

"Lucy," he said with a dreamy sound to his voice.

Oh yeah, I could tell that he had it bad. I smiled at him. "That's a pretty name."

"She's a pretty girl."

I felt a hesitation to him. Like something was bothering him or that he was withholding something. I cannot explain it but I get those types of feelings at times. Momma Rose says that she gets them too. Like that time when the phone rang. Momma Rose told me before she answered it that it was bad news. After she got off the phone she came and told me that a cousin of hers had been killed in a car accident.

Now I'm not saying that you can compare that feeling that Momma Rose had to the one I was having right now. I'm just saying that we Richards girls feel things. I guess I should say Marksberry girls because that's Momma's name before she married Daddy. Marksberry's her maiden name.

"Don't she like you?"

"Of course she likes me. Why wouldn't she like me?" Elvis asked, that leg of his bopping up and down.

"I'm asking is all. No need to get upset about it. Besides, she'd be crazy not to like you."

"You think so?" he asked.

"I know so. There's only one drawback as I can see."

"And what is that?" Elvis asked, but he picked up on the fact that I was only going to josh with him.

"That name. Where in the heck did your Momma come up with that?"

"Easy, you see Elvis is my daddy's middle name."

"What's his first name?" I asked.

"Vernon."

I looked him in the eye, unable to keep the smile from my lips. "She made the right choice. You certainly are not a Vernon."

We both broke out into laughter then and it was several minutes before either of us gained our composure. There were more than a few attempts that failed as one would look to the other and one or both of us would be laughing again.

I head a hand to my hurting side. "What time is it?"

Elvis looked at his watch. "Ten to midnight. I better get you back home."

"Don't you have to pick up Lucy?"

"I'm not going to let you walk home alone, May. It's not safe for a girl."

"I'll be okay," I said. "It's not that far."

"I don't know."

I knew I had to convince him. Sneaking back into the house would be way trickier than sneaking out. Not that I worried about Thelma but I knew there was a chance that Nick would be watching. He always seemed to be watching where I was concerned.

"How about you walk me to the top of the alley. You can watch me the rest of the way home from there."

"But—," he started to argue.

"But nothing. Nick might be at the house. He doesn't like you and if he actually catches you in the yard I don't know what he would do. I can do this."

"And what if he catches you?"

I shrugged. "I couldn't sleep and went for a walk."

"He probably won't believe you."

I stood up and face him. "Then you can tell me so in the morning."

Elvis looked like a man unhappy with his options. I tried making the pill go down a little smoother. "You know I'm right. It was my decision to meet you. If I get caught it should be me that gets the punishment."

Elvis pushed up off the bench. "Whatever you say, pet. I just hope I don't have to tell you I told you so."

"I couldn't agree with you more."

\*\*\*

*I made it,* was the first thought that ran through my head as I lowered the window back down to the sill. Once we made it to the alley we waved goodbye and I made my way through the shadow to my backyard. The house looked still and I couldn't see anyone walking around. I wasted no time getting my butt inside.

Once there I stopped and listened. I could hear Thelma still chatting away on the phone. I had really gotten away with it. I smile at the achievement. I changed into my nightgown, climbed into bed (all without walking Daisy), and slept better than I had in weeks.

# CHAPTER TWENTY

The next morning was Saturday and Momma Rose was home cleaning. When she was off from work she was like the other two who were late sleepers. But on days she decided to clean we were all awake at the crack of dawn with orders to make the house spic and span. After my late night with Elvis all I wanted was to sleep to eight and then have my morning with J.D.

Momma Rose made sure that didn't happen.

All morning beds were stripped, linens were changed, dishes were washed, floors were mopped. You get the drill. We worked and we worked hard. Not that Momma Rose was a slacker. She worked as hard or, in the case of Daisy, harder than any one of us.

We worked that morning so by the time the heat of the day settled in we would be finished. By noon we were all done and the thermometer outside said ninety-seven degrees. Thelma got cleaned up and left to go meet Eddie. Momma Rose and Daisy laid down for an afternoon nap, which left me all alone.

That didn't bother me much. I took a quick bath, brushed out my hair, and settled down to read the book I had gotten at the library. Only I did not get to read. I had barely gotten more than a paragraph when the phone rang. I leaned over the side of the couch and answered it.

"Hello?"

"Rose?"

It was Nick. I tried to sound impersonal. "No, May."

"Lord, girl, you sure do sound grown up like your Momma."

What do I say to that? I decided to ignore it. "Momma's napping right now. You want me to wake her up?"

There was a long pause and for a second I thought the operator disconnected the call. "No, no don't do that. You know how she is when you wake her."

"Okay," I said and started to hang the phone up.

"May."

I wanted to pretend that I did not hear him but I knew it would not work. I would just pay for it at a later date. I lifted the received back to my ear. "Yes?"

"Bring me over a glass of milk will you? I ran out this morning and would like some with my sandwich."

"I think we are out of milk too."

"That's funny. I saw full carton in there yesterday."

*Damn it.* "I'll check again."

"Two minutes. I want you standing at my front door in two minutes, you hear me?"

"Yes."

"Yes what?"

The power trip must have been a heady feeling. I was trapped. "Yes sir."

I went to the kitchen and poured the glass of milk. I then went out the front door and crossed the street. I felt nauseous and knew nothing good was about to happen. As I got to the porch I saw that the door was open behind the screen. A radio played country music in the background. I knocked on the screen door. No one answered so I knocked again. Only this time it was a little harder.

"May?" came Nick's voice.

"Yes…sir," I said. If you could choke on a word, I would have.

"You alone?"

"Yes."

"Come on in. The door's open."

I opened the screen up just enough to slip my body inside. My butt not quite completely out of the door frame kept the screen from latching shut. "I'll just sit this on the table for you–"

"Stay there."

I looked around Nick's house. Its layout was identical to mine. The biggest difference was that it lacked the personal touches. It lacked a feminine touch. I'm sure Momma Rose planned to right that when the time was right. The living room was immaculately clean. One could tell by looking that no children resided in the home. There were no juice stains on the carpet. None of the walls were dirty with little fingerprints or crayon marks. Nothing was out of place.

Except me. There was no doubt about it that I didn't belong here. I just didn't know how to go about getting away.

Nick came out from one of the back bedrooms. I guessed it was his bedroom given his state of undress. He was dressed in only pair of blue jeans. His shirt and shoes were gone and a white bath towel hung around his neck.

"Well, girl, are you just going to stand there? Shut the door and quit letting the flies in," he said, using the edge of his towel to wipe his face. "I got a little cleaned up. Your Momma hates it when I forget to shave. Sit down."

"I'm not planning on stay long," I say.

"Not planning on staying long? How would you know how long I plan on keeping you here?"

"If Momma Rose wakes up and finds me gone she's going to come looking for me."

Nick moved his head up and down like he was agreeing with me. "But she would never think to look here for you first. I'm guessing I could keep you busy all afternoon before she would show up here."

This had to be the weirdest conversation I had ever had in my life. What was he trying to do? Why wouldn't he just do it? My mouth went dry and my eyes begin to sting. Maybe that was why my mouth went dry. All of the moisture in my body was focusing on my eyes at the moment. I just prayed for it all to end.

Nick crooked a finger at me. "I just thought we could talk. You know, like you and your buddy Elvis."

I stood glued to the spot. I could not lead myself to the slaughter. I had done everything that Nick had asked of me. I would not do this. If he wanted to hurt me he would have to come and get me.

"You blind as well as deaf?" Nick got to his feet. Tossing the towel to the couch he made his way over. Stopping right in front of me. I kept my head level and stared straight into his chest. I did not want to look meek and hang my head but neither did I have the courage to look him directly in the eye.

I could hear him breathing. It was a bit faster than normal but not a pant. He placed his hands around my neck and used his thumbs to push my head up. I swallowed hard.

"Such a pretty little thing. Pretty, pretty little thing."

I closed my eyes and lips tightly as he put his lips to mine. I pushed his chest but he was bigger and stronger. All I could manage was a wiggle that made him laugh as he pulled back.

Nick took my hand and pulled me toward the couch. I dug my heels in to stop him. He glanced over his shoulder. "It's either the couch or the bedroom, sweetheart. It's all up to you how we take this. I bet Daisy wouldn't fight me this much."

Daisy. He was right. She would follow Nick anywhere. Daisy would be in over her head before she even began to suspect to that she was in trouble to begin with. I began walking.

"I think I've found your—what is it they call it? Your Achilles heel." Nick flopped down and pulled me down beside him. "You want to watch some television?"

I shook my head. Like everything else it did not really matter what I wanted. It was all an illusion to Nick. He jumped up and turned the set on. He adjusted the sound but it was louder than I would have liked. He went over to the desk and rummaged around in the drawer for a moment. When he returned to couch he sat a bowie knife on the arm farthest away from me.

He rested his one hand on the handle. "A little insurance just in case you decided you're going to scream and bring somebody over here."

I looked over at him. He read the fear in my eyes. "I'm not going to kill you, May."

I didn't believe him.

"But I can hurt you in ways you'd be ashamed to tell your momma about."

I believed that.

"Now," he said, "I'm going to touch you. Have you ever been touched by a man before?"

I shook my head.

"Not even that Presley boy?"

If this was not happening and Nick was another person I would inform him on just how wrong he was about Elvis. He's got it in his sick head that Elvis is like him. Which could not be further from the truth.

"No."

He touched the top of one of my thighs. "I know he wants to Spread your legs a bit, sweetheart."

When I did he slid his hand to the inside of my left thigh. He did not move it and we just sat there like that. I stared at the television without really seeing it.

"You like watching these shows?"

"No." Not that I knew what "shows" Nick was talking about. All I could think about was the hand that was on the inside of my thigh and what he would do next. When would he let me leave? What would Jack think if he were to see me now? I knew he would be as disgusted as I felt.

"See this ain't so bad, is it?" he said and began tapping his thumb, "I think we are going to get along just fine."

"What about Momma Rose?" The words came sailing out of my mouth before I could check them.

His thumb stopped. "What about her? I'm going to marry her."

"If you love Momma Rose then why do this to me?"

"I'm not doing anything to you, sweetheart. And I do love your Momma but this..." He moved his hand to my crotch and cupped me there, "this is what keeps me up thinking at night."

I closed my legs tight but that just kept his hand trapped where he wanted it. Something set off in me. Survival mode I guess because I grabbed at his hand and pulled but he didn't budge. I tried to move farther down the couch. Raising my legs I kicked at Nick. I don't know where I landed but I heard him grunt.

I was almost to my feet when he grabbed me around my waist and flung me backward. I landed on the couch flat on my back. Nick towered over me, his hand resting on the belt of his jeans.

"I tried doing this the nice way but you don't want that."

I tried to fight but he used his weight to hold me down. Not that he had to at that point. He laid the knife on the coffee table and I thought about what he said he would do. I never once screamed. Never tested the theory. I don't know why. I guess part of me just wanted him to give up. To say that I was too much trouble. Another part of me thought about Daisy. I couldn't let her go through this.

Nick removed his belt and unbuttoned his pants. I thought that he would lower them and pull his thing out but he didn't.

"Not yet, sweetheart. That would end things too soon. Pull your shirt up."

I think it was at that moment that something broke in me. I pulled the shirt up leaving me covered in only my white training bra with its tiny pink bow in the middle. I thought he might ask for me to remove that as well but he did not. Instead he bent my knees up and lowered his head to kiss my stomach.

I swallowed back vomit. After he was done kissing me there Nick settled himself between my legs and began touching and kissing my breasts. All of it over the bra at first. The material was soaked with his saliva and felt icky against my skin. I hated it. I hated him.

That first time could have lasted a few minutes or an hour. My mind checked out of the situation and I lost track of time. It was almost as if I left my body and was watching this happen to someone else. My brain could not process how I was laying half-naked being violated by Nick.

It was almost a relief when he pulled down my pants and put it inside of me. It hurt worse than anything I had ever felt before. I remembered that I couldn't scream so I bit my lip as the tears streamed down my face. I thought for sure that he would rip my small body in two with his repeated thrusts. Finally he fell against me and buried his face in my neck. I think he might have kiss me but I'm not really sure. It was over.

As I laid there all I could think about was how I was going to keep this from Momma Rose. I'm hot and sweaty, I must look a mess. How would I keep her from finding out what Nick had done to me? A little more time passed before he sat up on the sofa.

He lowered my shirt and handed me my shorts. I started to slip them on.

"I want you to go in there and take a shower before you get dressed."

There was a knock at the door. "Nick?"

It was Momma Rose. "Nick, open up. I need to talk to you."

"Momma," I said.

"I'll deal with your Momma. I won't let her in. I'll tell her I sent you on a few errands. You get in there wash yourself real good. You'll stay here until your hair is dry and you won't say a word. You hear me?"

I heard.

Another knock.

I grabbed up my clothes and shoes and ran to the back of the house. The last thing I heard before closing the bathroom door was Momma. "Have you seen May? I can't find her anywhere."

I shut the door and slid down the door. I buried my head on my knees. Half-naked, violated, bleeding, and hiding in a bathroom. It was the lowest point of my life.

# CHAPTER TWENTY

I thought it was going to be nightfall before Nick let me go home. After taking a shower, a hot one that left my skin red and blotchy from all the scrubbing I had done, he told me what to tell Momma Rose. I went to the grocery store and then to the hardware store to pick up a new flashlight and batteries. I then stopped by to pick up some roses for Nick to give Momma on their date tonight but the florist was already closed.

He didn't touch me "like that" again. Instead he cleaned up the mess we had made in the living room and showered again. When he got finished he fixed us both a sandwich. We didn't use the milk as it had be sitting out for over two hours by that point.

I did as I was told. It was easier that way. I sat, ate, and did not cause any problems. Sitting was hard. For not only did I hurt in the inside, Nick had also left some bruises on my hips, private area, and thighs. Thankfully my shorts covered the damage as I would hate to have to explain to Momma Rose why I had changed my clothes or worse yet the fingerprints that were on my body.

When Nick finally let me go he warned me one last time. "If your Momma comes over here with questions I'm going to know that you didn't keep our secret and all deals are off. You understand?"

"I understand."

I opened the screen door and walked out. The world looked exactly as it did when I entered hell. The sun was lower in the sky but it was shining. Birds were chirping, dogs barking, and I even heard kids playing. Nothing had changed and yet everything was different. The irony was lost not on me.

Momma Rose was in her bedroom getting ready for her date tonight when I got home. Thelma and Daisy were sitting at the table playing the card game war.

"Where have you been?" Thelma asked.

"I was helping Nick run errands," I said, pulling the dollar out of my pocket he had given me to show them, "he paid me to run to the market for him."

"May is that you?" Momma Rose yelled from her bedroom.

"Yes Momma, it's me," I yelled back. The sudden urge to cry was overwhelming. I fought to keep it under control.

Momma Rose stuck her head out the door and looked down the hall at me. Her shoulder was bare so I could tell that she was in the process of getting dressed. "What took you so long?"

"I stopped at the library before I made my stops for Nick. I'm sorry I didn't tell you where I was going. Nick said it was alright."

"It's fine. As long as Nick knew where you were," Momma Rose disappeared into her room again. "But don't get any ideas about running off like that again."

"I won't," I said and flopped down into the chair. Pain shot through my lower body. Thankfully I faced away from the table. The looked on my face had to be one of agony. I did not cry out but I must have tightened up because Thelma came over and sat on the couch.

"I wish you would have waited for me to get back from Eddie's," she whispered so Daisy and Momma Rose did not hear. "I know you don't like him."

"Hey, I got a dollar out of it," I tried to tease. Thelma just frowned. My anxiety grew as I realized that she didn't believe me. I knew to protect Daisy she had to believe me. She just had to. My heart pounded in my chest. I sure was giving the ole ticker a workout today.

"I want a dollar," Daisy said, coming over to sit by Thelma.

"I'll give you mine," I said, tossing the dollar onto Daisy's lap.

"That was mighty generous of you," Thelma said suspiciously.

"Thank you!" Daisy said, holding the dollar up to the light, "I know what I'm going to spend it on."

"What's that?" I asked, feigning interest in hopes of changing the subject.

"I'm going to buy a whole dollar's worth of penny candy."

"That's an awful lot of candy for a little girl," Momma Rose said, coming out of her room. She did a spin that sent her navy blue skirt twirling around her. "How do I look?"

"Pretty," Daisy said.

"You look nice," Thelma answered.

"Very nice Momma," I chimed in with a thrill I did not feel.

Momma Rose did not get a chance to give me a glance as there was a knock at the door.

"I'll get it," Daisy said, jumping up and running across the room.

"Daisy, stop running before you fall down and break your neck," Momma said.

Daisy stopped short of the door and pulled it open. "Nick," she screamed like she had not seen him in months instead of a day.

"There's my second favorite gal," he said, lifting her up into his arms. Daisy wrapped her arms around his neck and hugged him tight.

"I'll be ready in a minute," Momma Rose said, "I need to grab my purse."

Nick caught Momma Rose's hand and pulled her to his side. "You're not getting away with giving me a kiss, Momma," he said.

Standing there, holding Daisy and kissing Momma, Nick looked like any other family man. There was nothing that stood out about him. Momma Rose always told us that we needed to stay away from strangers. She said that strangers would hurt me and Daisy. I never had a stranger hurt me the way Nick did today. I am starting to see where Momma Rose is wrong about more and more things.

Nick put Daisy down and Momma went back to get her purse. Nick leaned up against the back of the chair I was sitting on. "Did May tell you what a helper she was to me today?"

"She sure did," Daisy said. "She even gave me the dollar you gave her."

"Now, sweetheart," he said, "you earned that money."

I chanced a glance at Thelma. She had a smile glued to her lips but I could see the question in her eyes. They seemed to say, I'm going to go with it but what is going on?

I smiled up at him. It was fake on my part but I hoped he bought it. "It's okay. I didn't mind helping out."

He believed me. I could see that the crazy son of a bitch thought I enjoyed what he did to me. He cracked a grin. "Well, then, I'll just have to find some more work for you."

"Me too," Daisy said.

"No," Thelma and I said in unison.

"But I want another dollar," Daisy whined.

"The work I have is for big girls, Daisy," Nick said. "But you know what?"

"What?"

"I bet I can talk your Momma into paying you an allowance for you helping out around here. What do you say?"

"I don't know," Daisy said, depressed.

"How about a quarter a week?"

"Oh boy! Do you really think so?"

"You just leave it up to me."

Momma Rose came back out with her new purse. "Leave what up to you? What are you people planning on me?"

Nick winked at Daisy who broke out into giggles. "Oh, nothing."

"Yeah. Nothing Momma Rose," Daisy rang in.

"I was just making a deal with the girls. I need some housekeeping done once a week. May said she would help."

"I don't know," Momma Rose said.

"May wants to. Don't you, May."

"I'll help," I said, not having any other choice in the matter.

"It shouldn't take a couple of hours a week. It will be good for her to earn her own money."

"Who am I to argue when you two are conspiring against me?" Momma Rose said with a smile of her own.

I knew what Momma Rose meant but the words could also take on a different meaning. As I watched them leave Nick playfully patted Momma Rose's behind and she swatted at his hand. They kissed again before finally heading out the door.

I didn't give Thelma a chance to question me I got up (as gingerly as possible) and locked myself in the bathroom. Turning on the light I stared at my reflection in the mirror. I did not know the girl staring back at me. I felt broken. I wanted to break something. I thought about the mirror but stopped. Mainly out of fear. Not the physical pain mind you, what happened at Nick proved that. I feared the questions.

I might be able to answer them one day…but not today.

I knew I had to break them up. If I didn't he would continue to hurt me. He wanted to marry Momma Rose. Once he did that, because I knew she would say yes, I would have to live with him. I would be at his mercy for everything until I was old enough to get out of the house. He would own me body and soul. That is, if he didn't kill me first.

# CHAPTER TWENTY-ONE

Nick and Momma Rose decided that it was best if I "cleaned" on Mondays. Momma Rose woke me when she left to go to work. I drug my feet as much as I could but Nick expected me by eight that morning. If it struck Momma Rose as odd that he would want me to come over so early she didn't say anything.

I ate my cereal inside at the kitchen table. That way I avoided J.D. I'm not sure why I wanted to avoid him other than shame. I thought if he took one look at my face that he would know that I was up to bad things. And the truth of the matter was that I felt I was up to something bad. I felt as if I was a part of the evil. Promptly at eight I made the march across the street and to my doom.

It was amazing how normal my life was when it wasn't Monday. I went to the movies, talked with Elvis, played with Daisy as if I did not have a care in the world. I felt as if there were two Mays. Monday May that survived Nick and the May that I displayed to everyone else. I didn't care for Monday May. I hated that I wasn't strong enough nor smart enough to stop Nick. I hated him and was beginning to hate Momma Rose because of him.

Why didn't she see what he was doing to me? Why was she blind to the monster she invited into my life? I doubt I will ever know.

July 4$^{th}$ approached before I realized. The 4$^{th}$ has always been my favorite holiday. I think it's mainly because my birthday is July 6$^{th}$ and we usually used the Fourth as my birthday party. What could be better than fireworks on your birthday?

This year the whole block decided to have a block party to celebrate. Since the holiday was on a Saturday, a day most people were off from work, everyone brought tables and lawn chairs into the front yards. Momma Rose called it a good old fashion barbeque.

We were all thankful that the weather cooperated. Louisville is known not only for its heat but its humidity. This day the temps hung in the mid-eighties and lower (read: not low) humidity. For most of the day everyone prepared for the evening's festivities. Momma Rose had me and Daisy out cleaning the lawn chairs and the card table she dug out of the closet while she and Thelma made potato salad, slaw, and a salad.

By late afternoon most people were sitting out on their lawns. A few friendly waves here and there but most people stuck to their own yards. Nick and a few of his buddies were standing around an old clunker with the hood popped up. From the beer in their hands it seemed that they were doing more posturing than actual mechanical work on the machinery.

Even Elvis joined in on the fun. J.D. was manning the grill while Vera arranged things on the picnic table the men had brought from the backyard. Elvis himself sat with his back to the table strumming on his guitar. People stopped what they were doing and listened. I wish he would have sung a few lines but Elvis seemed content getting lost in the music. After Daisy and I finished our chores we walked over to him. Daisy began dancing while I stood there.

After about a half dozen songs he put the guitar on the bench seat beside him. Daisy moaned her displeasure. "More."

"I've got to let my fingers rest a little bit," he went on when it looked as if Daisy would continue to object, "That way I can play for my best girl later."

Daisy beamed when Elvis gave her a wink. That was the way the evening went. There was laughing, teasing, jokes, and storytelling. I sat on our front lawn and watched as people from all walks of life communicated. I do not think that I felt a part of them. It was more that I was observing them to see how they worked. Kind of like when Daisy and I would trap lightning bugs in an old mason jar. I watched these people to see how they ticked.

As the sun set I noticed how Momma Rose drank more beer. This afternoon she nursed one drink for hours. Now, though, as the sun began to set, inhibitions lowered for Momma Rose and she had downed three beers in the last half hour. I guess the darkness made her feel like no one was watching. I watched, though, and did not care for it at all. Momma Rose flitted from neighbor to neighbor flirting with any man in sight. The women quickly found excuses to draw their men away from Momma. She could care less as she moved on to another man.

As she laughed and drank I noticed that she kept glancing over at Nick. He was still surrounded by his buddies and pretended not to notice. I knew he was pretending but I didn't know why. As far as I knew, he and Momma Rose were getting along fine. They were not one to fight much anyway. It seemed that I was missing a very important piece to the puzzle.

Thelma came and sat beside me. After we had set everything up she had went and changed into a new outfit she had purchased for this occasion. It was a pair of denim pants cuffed at the bottom and a white button up blouse. With her hair pulled back in a ponytail she looked every inch the All American girl.

"Tonight looks like there are going to be more fireworks than the ones in the sky," she said.

"What's going on between those two anyway?" I asked.

"Trust me, you don't want to know."

"Did they get into a fight?"

Thelma took a deep breath and slowly released it. "Something like that."

Sometimes I think that Thelma wanted me to drag stuff out of her. That she got some kind of enjoyment out of it. I turned in my chair and stared at her. If she wanted to tell me she would.

"You're too young to hear it."

I narrowed my eyes and crossed my arms.

"I'm serious May."

I did not say a word. I continued looked at her.

It took another sixty seconds for her to crack. "Aunt Rose found out that Nick's been fooling around with another girl."

My heart plummeted to the bottom of my stomach and sighed in relief. I wanted to turn away but then Thelma would know that something was wrong. She knew how much I hated Nick (if not why) and knew that I would love hearing this type of gossip. Maybe this would break them up.

From the look on her face Thelma and Momma Rose neither suspected me. "Who? How did she find out?"

"Aunt Rose found a present in Nick's closet from Snyder's department store. It was wrapped up in some fancy wrapping and she thought it was for her. So she opened it."

"What was inside?" I had a suspicion that I knew. Nick had taken to buying me things and keeping them at his house. Mostly clothes and such that should belong to a much older woman.

"From what I heard it was a gold I.D. bracelet with the letter M engraved on it. A real expensive one too."

"Maybe it was my birthday present," I offered. I knew it was my birthday present. Nick had often told me in the last few weeks that he was going to get it for me. He said it was to "remind me" that I belonged to him.

"That's what Aunt Rose thought to until she read the card."

My stomach did a nauseous flip that threatened to make the hotdog I ate earlier reappear. "What did it say?"

Thelma leaned closer. "To my beloved M, may you always feel my love for you," Thelma sat back. "Aunt Rose lost it and tore the place up. When Nick got home he told her the bracelet was for his mother but Rose didn't believe him."

Of course my mother didn't believe him. She was no idiot. "What else happened?"

"They got into one hell of a fight. Apparently Momma Rose found some of the woman's stuff in an old trunk next to the attic door in Nick's bedroom."

I nodded. I knew the trunk well. It was my trunk.

"Did you ever see it when you were cleaning?"

I shook my head. "I rarely cleaned Nick's room." Which was not too far from the truth. The only thing I would do was change the sheets after he and I were done.

"Well, needless to say, it was full of sexy nightgowns and such that Aunt Rose knew the trunk could not belong to his mother."

If the ground were to open up and swallow me whole I would be eternally grateful. I looked down at the ground but alas it wasn't meant to be. I told myself to be thankful for small miracles that Momma Rose had not figured out that the other woman was in fact her own little girl.

"Nick finally admitted to it and told her he was sorry he hurt her."

"He did?"

"Yep, but you know Aunt Rose. She won't be happy until she finds out who it is. That's why she's flirting with every man here. I'm just afraid that she's going to sleep with a few of them to get back at Nick."

Normally I would not be afraid for that. Momma Rose thought too much of herself to be another man's one night stand. But looking at her now I wasn't so sure. She was talking to J.D. and even flirting with him. A man old enough to be her father! Thankfully he didn't seem interested in the goods Momma Rose offered.

I'm guessing by the end of the night it would take all three of us girls to get her into the house.

\*\*\*

Even with Momma Rose's antics I enjoyed the next few hours. Daisy, Thelma, and I laid a blanket out on the lawn and watched the fireworks. Eddie and Jack came by toward the end and we had fun just sitting there talking. Jack laid on his side beside me. As the fireworks sailed overhead he took my hand in his. It startled me. I looked from our joined hands to his eyes and knew.

This was the boy I was meant to find.

This was the man I was destine to love.

The look in his eyes told me he felt the same thing. When our lips met this time there were literally fireworks. This was love and I knew I would have to share my ugliness with him. But not just yet I told myself. Not this night. This night I got the magic.

After the show people began cleaning up and heading inside for the night. Thelma, Eddie, Jack, Daisy, and I walked over to talk J.D. and Elvis. Thankfully Momma Rose had finally given up trying to make Nick jealous and had went inside and promptly fell asleep or passed out on the couch. I had just gotten Daisy down for the night and had started on the kitchen clean up when the door opened.

Nick.

# CHAPTER TWENTY-TWO

Nick had been drinking but as usual he was far from drunk. Maybe a little sloppy you would say.

"Momma's on the couch," I said, more as a warning than anything else. I hoped that his fear of being caught was more than his appeal to have a go at me.

"I guess you heard what happened?"

I nodded and moved away from him. "So what are you going to do now?"

Nick stood on the other side of the island. "I'll make it up to Rose. Make her believe that she is the only one."

He pulled a small ring box out of his pocket. "I think this will work."

It didn't shock me. I knew this was his plan. He would marry Momma Rose and we would all live together.

"You know she'll say yes. She loves me even after finding out what she did about us."

"There is no us," I said. "There's you and what you do to me."

Nick laughed softly. "What I do to you? Are you serious little girl? You loved every minute of it."

"I did not," I said, my voice cracking as I tried to keep it at a whisper. "You hurt me."

Nick began stalking me around the counter. His drunken steps not quite as stealthy as he would normally be. "I only hurt you when you needed discipline. When you needed guidance. All the other times you enjoyed yourself."

"I didn't," I said more to myself than to him. But he was right. My body did like the attention. Especially when he would rub me down with his hands or his mouth. It confused me how my body liked something so horrible. So despicable.

"See," Nick said, "I see you thinking there. You liked it when I made you feel like a woman. Hell girl, I taught you well. And don't think that I didn't see you with that boy tonight. I thought it was the Presley boy I had to worry about. But I'm thinking that it's Eddie's kid brother that's going to be the bother."

"He's nothing for you to worry about."

"That's a good thing," Nick said. "From what I hear he's nothing more than a troublemaker. I wouldn't take too kindly to him dating my daughter."

*My daughter*. Had Nick really uttered those words? His daughter? The light flipped to red in my head and the filter to my mouth was blown off. "Your daughter? Is that what I am to you?"

"Lower your voice."

I was beyond caring what he wanted. Of being scared of him. Momma wouldn't hear me. She was three sheets to the wind. Thelma was gone and hopefully Daisy was sleeping the sleep of the dead. I also knew Nick would make me pay for anything I said or did but at this point I was just mad.

"Why, *Daddy*?" I said, stressing the second word, "You don't want anyone to know what you did to me? What you do to me?"

I'm surprised that I managed to stay on my feet the slap was that forceful. Pain shot through the side of my face and burned my skin. It was enough to give Nick the upper hand again. He grabbed me by the arm and pulled me close. "I'm done playing games with you, sweetheart."

I spit in his face and fought to get free. The next thing I knew I was face down against the island. I couldn't scream because the wind had been knocked out of me. He slammed my head against the countertop. Pain exploded then and made the slap seem like a playful tap. I felt him lowering my shorts and kicking my legs apart. The tips of my toes barely reaching the ground. I felt his hand undoing his belt as he pressed against my butt. I pushed at the counter but was helpless to stop him. He grabbed my wrists and held them at the small of my back.

He leaned over me and whispered against my ear. "Don't worry, sweetheart. I'll make sure you don't have any mixed feelings about this time."

"Nick?"

The voice was not mine. I opened my eye that was half way swollen shut to see Daisy standing in the doorway. Her brown eyes wide as saucers.

"Go back to bed," Nick told her but she didn't move. He twisted my arm. "Tell her to go to bed. Remember our deal."

"May?" Daisy said, her lower lip quivering in fear.

I hoped that the counter hid the fact I was naked below the waist and the true intention of what Nick planned to do to me. "You need to go back to bed Daisy. I'll talk to you about it later."

"Are you sure? Your eye is all black and swole up."

I tried to nod. "I'll be okay."

She did not want to leave me and the fact was I did not want her to leave but Daisy turned and went back to bed. Once she was gone I rested my forehead to the countertop.

"That's a good girl.," Nick smacked me on ass. His hand went back to his belt. "I hope she realizes what you do for her."

"I hope she never does," I whispered against the marble.

The back door crashed back against the frame.

"What the fuck?" Nick said, moving away from me. I reached down and pulled my pants back into place.

Elvis. Elvis was there and madder than I had ever seen him. I stumbled around him as he made his way to Nick. I saw Elvis punch him several times. Each landing with a thud. Nick fell to the ground but Elvis lifted him up and pounded him once again.

A flood of feelings rushed through me and my legs crumbled. The ground rushed up to meet me but I was caught before I hit the ground. Arms enveloped me.

"I got you," Jack said, kissing my temple, "I've got you."

Thelma was there too. And Eddie. And Daisy. They were right there with me. My family. All but Momma Rose. The tears I had held at bay for way too long began rolling down my cheeks. Jack held me tighter while Thelma touched my brow. When she garnered a look at Nick she looked to Eddie.

"You better get him before he kills that son of a bitch."

I watched from the safety of Jack's arms as Eddie stopped Elvis. The truth was Eddie was the only one big enough to stop Elvis. Nick was in an unconscious heap on the ground. It should have been a surreal moment for me but it wasn't. The moment was all too real.

"I need to stand up," I said to no one in particular. Thelma helped me to my feet and pulled me into her embrace. "I'm so sorry May. I thought I was the only one he tried to bother. If I had known I would have killed him myself."

"I know," I said.

I took a seat at the table. Nick stood behind me and Daisy clung to my side. It's funny the embarrassment I always felt when it came to Nick did not bother me. It was still there mind you, but not as bad as one would expect. All of these people had seen me at my worst and I knew that if I asked they would carry it to their grave. There was no judgment, just family.

Elvis stopped at the sink and washed off Nick's blood before coming over to me. He did not admonish me or placate me. He smiled at Daisy. "You got a gem of a sister, pet."

Daisy threw her arms around my neck and hugged me tight. "I'm sorry, May. I just didn't know what to do."

Jack tousled Daisy's hair. "You did good, love."

"You did the right thing," I said between sniffles.

"What in the world?" Momma Rose said coming into the kitchen. She looked from the beaten and battered me to the unconscious Nick. While some of her drink had worn off it was clear that she wasn't one hundred percent on what was going on.

Thelma told Momma Rose what happened in the most simplest and tasteful words possible. Her face was unreadable as Thelma finished. She walked over to Nick and bent down to say something that none of us across the room could hear. The only thought I had was "She chose him. She knows the truth and she chose him."

Momma Rose stood up and ran a hand through her tangled hair. Then she began kicking Nick. First it was the stomach and then as he tried to get out of the way she kicked him blindly. "You fucking son of a bitch. You asshole—," her string of vulgarity went on until she was out of both breath and energy.

When she was finished Momma Rose turned to me and the strong momma I had always known was gone. Tears ran her mascara down her cheeks and she looked years older than she had just the day before. In the weeks that followed we would talk about everything that happened that night. In detail, in triplicate when the nightmares came. But right then at that moment Momma Rose did the only things I needed her to. She believed me.

## EPILOGUE

I would like to tell you that Nick went to prison for what he did to me. But in 1953 that was not going to happen. A neighbor called the police that night and they showed up a few minutes after Momma Rose stopped kicking Nick. After hearing my harrowing story they hauled Nick to jail. Funny thing, when the police asked who had did the number on Nick Eddie took the blame. No one else he said. The cops believed him and arrested Eddie as well. I asked him years after why he took the fall and he said, "Elvis was too pretty and there was no way the cops would believe that Jack could do such damage."

Nick was charged with assault and did three months in county jail. I don't know what happened to him after that. He moved out of the house across the street and out of all of our lives. Daisy and I lived in that house until we both got married. She was the one that went to college and earned a Masters Degree in Education. She eventually married a nice preacher man and moved to farm. They had three children and a bunch of goats.

Thelma and Eddie married each other three times. The last one seemed to stick and they've been married over twenty years.

Momma Rose, wracked with guilt, waited another decade before she dated again. He was a nice older man with kids and grandkids. They didn't seem to have much in common but somehow it worked for them. I love and miss both of them.

Now on to Jack. Jack didn't leave Louisville when he planned. He waited a little over a year. Till my eighteenth birthday to be exact. That afternoon we boarded a train to California. For the next three years we traveled the United States. When we were finished we came home and started our family. Our lives, while not perfect, have been happy.

As for Elvis, the man who became the King, you might know how his story turned out. But now you know that for one summer he was a young boy with a dream. A boy who was a good friend and helped save me when I couldn't save myself.

Made in the USA
Columbia, SC
23 October 2023